YOUR LOVE AND MY STORY

A tit for tat, the other way around

HARISH PANDEY

First published in Dec 2019 by

Becomeshakespeare.com

Wordit Content Design & Editing Services Pvt Ltd
Unit - 26, Building A -1, Nr Wadala RTO,
Wadala (East), Mumbai 400037, India
T: +91 8080226699

Wordit Art Fund helps deserving authors publish
their work by providing monetary support.
To apply for funding, please visit us at
www.BecomeShakespeare.com

Disclaimer

ISBN - 978-93-89759-60-0

DEDICATION

"TO THE FRIENDSHIP,

THAT GROWS WITH YOU

AND WITHIN YOU"

ABOUT THE AUTHOR

HARISH PANDEY (29, single)

Harish belongs to a family of Defense personnel as his father served and retired from the Border security force and his only sibling, his older brother is serving in the Indian Navy. He is a native of the Kumaon region of Uttarakhand and spent his entire childhood in Kashipur Uttarakhand where he also completed his primary education. His parents still reside there. He moved to Delhi in 2007 for his technical education (engineering) and since then he has stayed in Delhi and has been employed in the Delhi Metro Rail Corporation (DMRC).

This is his first book, which also happened to him in a very unconventional way, the story of which he has already mentioned in the 'PREFACE'. Writing a book is definitely a 'no-nonsense thing' and therefore it takes a lot more than what is estimated but having it completed in a proper way gives the ultimate joy of adding a feather in the author's cap. He hopes he can add some more.

Harish loves playing sports especially cricket and football. He loves writing short stories and poems in

Hindi as well.

FACEBOOK PAGE: Your Love & My Story

INSTAGRAM AND TWITTER HANDLE: agekraze

EMAIL: ylams.hp61@gmail.com

ACKNOWLEDGEMENTS

"Without generosity, heart is merely a pumping organ," someone wrote this, hopefully you'll find it later.

But true it is.

And acknowledgements are the vital part of this generosity.

And therefore I want to send a big hug to everyone who I had memories with, who somehow knowingly or unknowingly touched me with their love and support towards me and those who inspired me to keep going and made me create this book (obviously unknowingly), which is right now in your hands.

So let's start from the one and only Almighty who blessed me to start and finally complete this book. I will always be grateful to THEE for everything.

My own college gang Amardeep (my roomie), Kundan, Manoj, Sawai and Shushil with whom I've experienced some actual moments that I have mentioned in this book.

Bhuppi, one more important member of our gang, who still never misses an opportunity to get jealous of me (intentionally :)) and makes me feel special in his exaggerated way of appreciation every time we get in touch. Well, appreciation does work as motivation and brings positivity to a situation where one finds himself/ herself in doubts.

Special mention to my school friend Kapil Kapri, who read the manuscript in no time and was too excited to get this book published. He treated this book as his baby and kept me hopeful in terms of marketing and publicity of the book during the initial phase.

Team at the Becomeshakespeare.com

Pooja Dutt- Senior publishing consultant who brought this special grant to me.

Sameer Ambildhok- Project manager who took care of my work to refine it to the purest form.

Anagha Bailur- My editor. I wrote it and she made sure to deliver everything exactly the way I wanted to say it.

A team of professionals! For some debutant like me they kept it smooth and simple.

Last but not the least, my family. I was keeping them out of it deliberately because like everyone else they too were unaware that 'something like this' was going on in my mind until I apprised them with 'the letter of intent' from one publishing house.

They were too proud of me, especially my mother just with that 'letter'. Making your family proud is ultimately one of the biggest achievements in life. It gives you satisfaction of some different level and that is why I want to give them a big hug for making me feel 'proficient'.

PREFACE

Writing a novel and thinking of writing a novel are two completely different things.

"I am good at delivering one-liners, great at using puns and a master in taking one to an emotional journey with surprised ups and downs through my narrative of seeing the other sides of the stories."

Or at least, I used to think so. I genuinely believe I am a creative guy who always looks forward to find/create some random beautiful and practical sequences and try to weave a sensible story with them. That's what an author does. So I too had some sequences in my mind for a very long time but I never thought of bringing them together for two strange reasons;

A)   I believed that when I can think of it so naturally, then it won't be that much troublesome to pen it down. So I can do it whenever I want to.

B)   And even if I start it and have it completed someday then also what's the big deal. I am not sponsored.

But then one fine day, I somehow started writing. I guess I got a cool, spiral-bound diary from my office and to use it personally, I decided to write. Yep I started it off that way. And with that first few pages I had written, I got to know very convincingly that thinking it and doing it and then sticking to it is not everyone's cup of tea.

I started writing the second chapter first which was the first chapter until I was struck with the idea of giving a twist to the tale. I wasn't sure of going much ahead in the process and therefore I would seldom pay a visit to it (also that lack of sponsors and a bit laid back attitude of mine towards this). But as all the characters got into their skins perfectly and the story picked up pace, I started feeling more like living in a world created of my own. And that's the beauty of being a creator especially an author. It all depends on you and your writing, how gracefully you do justice with the characters (I feel I did). I literally felt like what's next to develop in the story to do complete justice with it.

A good writer is like a good chef who makes you fall in love with what he cooks the best along with satisfying your appetite and taste-buds. My quest for best and relatable stuff for my story was going high and high. And then I stuck to a point which was kind of an anticlimax.

I had the characters to relate with. I had the content with real driving force and I also had the perfect ending to it. But what I missing on was the 'separation part'. How to justify a 'larger than life' friendship to go into 'bad blood' and then a 'never coming back together' situation.

Quoting directly from the very famous and one of my favorite movie 'THE PRESTIGE'

"Every great magic trick consists of three parts or acts. The first part is called "The Pledge". The magician shows you something ordinary: a deck of cards, a bird or a man. He shows you the object. Perhaps he asks you to inspect it to see if it is indeed real, unaltered, normal. But of course… it probably isn't. The second act is called "The turn". The magician takes the ordinary something and makes it do something extraordinary. Now you are looking for the secret… but you won't find it, because of course you are not looking. You don't really want to know. You want to be fooled. But you wouldn't clap yet. Because making something disappear isn't enough; you have to bring it back. That's why every magic trick has a third act, the hardest part, the part we call "The Prestige".

So basically, I had "The Pledge", I had the "The Prestige" what I didn't have that time was "The Turn". How to disappear one of the protagonists which somehow caused separation to every other character linked with him, was the big deal for me. As I had not been coming up with any appropriate sequence and justified reason, so I let it be (because I had no deadline to follow as I was not sponsored ;)).

Meanwhile I somehow managed to send some chapters of my manuscript to several publishing houses (who considers unsolicited manuscripts). And as I mentioned earlier I already had the perfect ending to the story (that 'prestige' thing was structured in my mind till then), to reconcile the protagonists in a surprising way. So I gave my best shot to it.

It took almost one month to get a positive response from one of the publishing houses I sent my sample chapters to. They really liked my work and therefore sent me 'Letter of Intent' along with their mail. They wanted my complete manuscript within one week for evaluation purposes. Like I said, appreciation is one of the biggest motivators and it really boosted my approach towards "The Turn" part and finally got away with 'no sponsor-excuse'. As a result of which, I completed the rest of my manuscript in two days only.

I sent it and got approved. Until that 'Letter of Intent', I didn't let anyone know about all this. My family was the first to know and obviously they were too happy for me.

CHAPTER 1

"AN ENVELOPE WITH A CHOCOLATE"

2016, PRESENT DAY

(A COUPLE OF HOURS EARLIER)

LOCATION: Within around 50kms radius of Chandigarh

(INSIDE THE CHAIR CAR COACH OF TRAIN "NDLS JANSHATABDI")

"Seat numbers 60, 61, ticket please," the Traveling Ticket Examiner (TTE) of the train said to the passengers of respective seats.

"Seat number 61," the respective seat allotted to that passenger said showing the ticket confirmation message she had received on her mobile through IRCTC (Indian Railway Catering and Tourism Corporation Limited).

"Radhika Thapar?" the TTE read the name from the printed list in his hand in order to confirm and looked at her.

"Yes, sir." The girl with the most beautiful smile replied in assent.

"Please show me your proof of identity ma'am," the TTE asked performing his duty and kept looking at her. The girl wearing a capped sleeve black top in floral print with a brown palazzo over her well-toned body adjusted her hair while opening the handbag.

"Just a second," the girl replied and peeped into her handbag to pick the identity proof.

"Here you are, sir." She quickly said as if she herself wasn't happy to keep him waiting and handed him her AADHAR CARD.

"Thank you, ma'am," the TTE said and returned it to her as soon as he confirmed it.

While putting it back into her handbag the girl spotted a C4 sized envelope, inside the bag. She immediately picked it out and checked. The envelope was tightly sealed and also a large size chocolate was tied to it with an adhesive tape. She turned it around and acted without losing a second as she found some relevant clue on its reverse side. The very next moment, she dialled a number and eagerly waited for the line to connect.

"Mihir, what's this envelope all about?" She asked as the receiver at the other end said 'HELLO'.

"Oh! I forgot to tell you about it," the male voice responded.

"I told you that we'll buy some gift together from there

itself, then why did you purchase it?" She said reminding him of their earlier agreement.

"Yeah Radhika but....," he replied to provide a justification but was not allowed to complete it.

"Aren't you coming over there tomorrow? Is that it?" She threw her preconceived notions as a question at him.

"I will." He kept his reply shorter and faster in order to not get cut off midway again.

"No, you won't otherwise you wouldn't have done this. You always do this." Feeling hopeless she announced the verdict and hung up the phone in anger.

She adjusted her hair again which while talking, got displaced from where they were supposed to be. Her cell phone rang in a second or two just after she cut the call. She saw and then carelessly chose the option 'Reject'. The same process was repeated for two more times until the caller himself gave up on the idea of calling.

"Boys are just like this, especially boyfriends." The co-passenger of the same-sex and of almost the same age, at berth number 60 said sharing her experience with a recently angered Radhika.

Radhika stared at her making an indifferent expression on her face. She was about to reply or even precisely, shout at her but before that, her cell phone beeped again. It was a text message this time from the same Mihir. She opened it and read it twice before deciding to dial on that number.

"No, not all actually and excuse me, please." She replied to her co-passenger while putting the cell phone to her ear.

"THE NUMBER YOU HAVE DIALED IS SWITCHED OFF. PLEASE TRY LATER." She got an answer from the network operator on the behalf of their customer at the designated number.

She impatiently tried a few more times but wasn't able to change the end result. She wasn't able to help herself out of it and therefore eventually opened the SMS INBOX in her cell phone and checked the message again. She seemed in some sort of indefinite confusion as she wasn't able to look away from the envelope which she was already holding in her hand. And in the process of making a decision over what to do and what not, she finally untied the chocolate from the envelope by removing the adhesive tape over it and putting her confusion aside she chose to consume chocolate.

****

CHAPTER 2

PRESENT DAY, (RIGHT NOW)

"SOME 260 KMs AWAY FROM CHANDIGARH"

"Well Begun is Half Done".

Sounds very motivating & makes the equation look easy to accomplish. But believe me, these preachings and sayings are just some superb quotes to read and listen, until you confront them yourself and, while going through the process, they turn out into real-time sufferings, restiveness, trauma & many more not-so-good emotions.

But the beginning is always the hardest thing to get going from a no motion position, especially for someone like me who was a pure novice or just a debutant, in better words.

'When I can write a complete book, which took almost three-fourths of a year & my complete peace of mind then why can't I hold my nerves for some more time? Just a few questions that I need to answer & I will be done. "And that's why I penned down this book" is the best answer for anything which I don't feel like actually answering.' I was continuously giving myself that talk to keep me cool & motivated.

I was definitely well prepped & purposefully equipped with my answer shields for the upcoming rapid fire as I knew I was on the target radar of the student audience sitting in front of me, in a whopping amount.

YES! I was at the book launch event at a college, at *my* college. Well, this book launch event was also mine, actually. I mean I have become a writer by chance & now was the time to answer the world questioning why have I become one?

DEL-I-E-T, pronounced as *'Delight'* & decoded as DELHI INSTITUTE OF ENGINEERING & TECHNOLOGY located in the suburbs of the National Capital, which promises and asserts in their advertisements, to evolve their students into an Engineer, has actually produced a writer. And if someone came up with this thoughtful question, it would be the worst thing I would have to encounter. I would really fall short of words for that career destroying question. And eventually, they would sum up how bad a writer I am, one who doesn't have wit. Along with my book, it would also be fatal for the reputation of the college, I thought. A single question could screw me over and everything related to me and sadly, I would become the first writer in the history to get thrown out of the fraternity for my first & only book because of such an unusual cause.

I knew I was over-thinking & overrating all that promotional activity but to be very honest, I was sweating bullets in a fully air-conditioned hall.

Fortunately, I was sharing that stage along with my very generous publisher Mr. Bhargava & the hope of my rainy days, Professor Bhatiya, who also happened to be my then H.O.D, and because of whose crappy idea, I was convinced to write this book.

Fortunately, he was also hosting that event, which more or less brought me a tad sigh of relief. Professor Ramesh Bhatiya, was a very jovial person, aged around 45 years. Despite his growing age, he didn't let the child inside him grow. He was still there, wrapped under a 6 feet long & 80 kg weighing body. Besides holding a Ph.D. in Electronics Engineering, he was also a great motivational speaker, who solely believed in motivating and not in raising false hopes. And convincing some non-writer like me, to pen down a book could easily explain how influential he could be!I was purely blessed that I got him as a mentor in my life.

"SILENCE! SILENCE! SILENCE!"

Professor Bhatiya more requested than yelled at the students who were more interested in discussing their own fiction rather than listening to my tragic tale of becoming a writer.

Although it was Sunday, the official rest day of the college, there was barely any space vacant to fill in that uber-spacious auditorium. Frankly, I wasn't expecting that hall to be jam-packed with such an enthusiastic crowd. Recently our college had started two new engineering courses leading to B TECH degrees in Computer Science & Engineering and another in Mechanical Engineering. Earlier, it only used to offer three courses that were Electronics & Telecommunications, Electrical, and Information Technology. The increased crowd was the result of increased courses, I thought in my head.

I kept wandering in the valley of notions until Professor wore his shoes of an anchor and commenced.

"Guys, it is always a matter of immense pride and honour for a teacher to see his students evolving personally as well as professionally. And, believe me, I am feeling the same while enunciating the name of one of my favourite students of all time who has recently turned into a writer. As we all know, we are gathered here for the book-launch event of this debutant writer, Vishesh Pratap Singh, who is also the alumnus of our esteemed college. And being his teacher, I am on cloud nine because of his out of the box effort. He was doing exceptionally well in his job as a Senior Engineer in a reputed company, but he finally quit that to devote his entire time to this book. I have already read the manuscript and then the printed version too and I must say he has it in him. I personally wish that he comes out with flying colours and achieve greater heights. More power to this creative genius!"

The professor was busy in introducing me to the audience in his unique style with heaps of praises. But I interrupted him a bit early before he could have formally requested me to share my feelings on that auspicious occasion. It was a deliberate interruption from my end as I soon realised the textbook style of addressing & answering would surely make me fall short of words and hence I thought of starting off unconventionally.

"Sorry sir, for the interruption and a big thank you, for the way you introduced me to this youngest set of engineers. But guys don't misinterpret his speech about me as a tool to mutiny. Nonetheless, congratulations to all of you as you have chosen to study one of the toughest & greatest courses on this planet. And believe me, you all are in safe hands of these phenomenal minds, teaching & mentoring you to learn Engineering with ease. Well, life today is a sheer glimpse of engineering and you guys yourself have boldly chosen Engineering as life. My best wishes are with you. Keep aspiring & keep doing the good work. Stay blessed.

"And Bhatiya sir, like always I need one more favour from you. Please don't request me to say few words about the book. I already had written a hell of a lot of them." I obliged keeping my speech short and simple.

Claps, Shouting, Hooting and Whistling ensued!

My statement got a warm response which literally meant, the audience who were mostly students, had accepted me and my proposal. Apart from these younger kids, the *gang* was there, sitting on the first row with the Dean & a few other professors and kind of pseudo-complimenting me. That was the only time I witnessed them in the first row at college ever and that too along with faculty. Well, friends *are* like this. They have a tendency of creating a fun-zone during wartime and at your wedding, they never miss an opportunity to make you feel like an asshole. 'How to screw a friend, in the best possible way?' is something every close friend knows and Siddhant, Lucky & Anshuman were leaving no stone unturned in proving it.

"HAHAHA, No issue champ. But have some mercy on your publisher too. After all, he has invested a hefty amount in it." Bhatiya sir said laughingly.

"Sure sir. I owe him for that." I said conformably.

"Guys lemme tell you something interesting about this book, not exactly about the content of the book but about its making. Are you patient enough to hear it?" I said while firmly holding up my mike and stood up from the couch I was sitting upon.

"YES! YEAH! YUP! SURE!" the crowd positively and enthusiastically replied in different words.

"This whole idea of book writing was of our most beloved professor, Mr. Bhatiya who injected it into me through his distinguished and well-known oratory. He suggested me to do so when I once went to him to seek advice regarding stability in my personal life. Now don't get shocked with this strange solution of treating a personal problem. This book will take you through all, which I already went through, alone and clueless. So I eventually agreed to his bizarre but optimistic piece of advice. Penning down a book was really a big deal in itself for someone like me, but raising monetary fund to publish it, was the biggest hurdle of all. I mean, no established publisher would love to risk his hard-earned money in publishing a book of a first-time writer or worse, a by-chance writer who just wanted to make peace with his life by writing about his personal life. One just needs guts and a big heart to glorify his gamble.

And then Mr. Anil Bhargava, well-known publisher & distributor of SWASTIK publications, and also a consistent distributor to our college, came forward to rescue me out of this problem. Professor Bhatiya who is a good friend of Mr. Bhargava recommended my story to him. Like me, Mr. Bhargava is also a first timer in publishing a fiction. I am not completely sure if my story won him over or not but the way Bhatiya sir convinced him with his vision, did the trick for me."

I took a pause and then further added.

"I am really grateful to both these gentlemen without whose mental and financial support, this book would neither be planned nor published."

I finished my speech on a bit of an emotional note but the crowd rewarded me with an overwhelming response.

The entire hall reverberated with a round of applause.

Suddenly, Mr. Publisher stood up from the couch that we were sharing and signalled me to hand him over the mike. I, without losing a second, complied. I behaved as if I really owed him.

"These writers really know how to mesmerize one. Isn't it?" Mr. Bhargava commenced with a complimenting statement.

"But perhaps they don't know, a true businessman never thinks from his heart. After all, money does matter in this materialistic world." He added further and laughed.

"But, But, But! .... along with a good businessman, I am also a good human being and that's why I don't believe in taking credit for the things which I don't deserve solely. So allow me to make a small but really very vital disclosure, right here right now."

Mr. Bhargava who didn't go with the image of the mysterious James Bond had something big to reveal. Something which I wasn't aware of, probably at all!

"Ramesh Bhatiya, your most blue-eyed professor and a very dear friend of mine, is actually a dark horse. I am sure, he won't appreciate me for doing this but as a friend I think, I should let you all know. He has invested 50% of the share in this book & according to that, for this book he has officially become my partner too, which was the most crucial reason, why I got ready to publish this book under my publications."

"And the irony is nobody knew it, not even our writer Mr. Vishesh Pratap Singh."

The audience, unlike me, didn't show any kind of shocking response. I guess they took it more like a publicity stunt, which was actually not.

"What is he saying, sir? Did you really….?" I whispered into the ears of Bhatiya sir who was sitting on a black leather throne shaped chair, next to me.

"Yeah, I was about to tell you, after this event."Bhatiya sir tried to evade the situation.

"But why sir, Why would you do such a favour for me? You already gave me a big shock earlier." I asked being emotional and reminded him of his shocking power.

"Not favouring you, son. I am just doing my bit." He said calmly & tapped my shoulder.

"Excuse me." He added immediately as his cell phone rang.

He stood up & went a few steps behind our seats. After talking for a few moments whispering, he came back to his seat.

Until then, Mr. Bhargava was also done with his speech, which was more like some game-changing tips on business etiquettes, towards the last. Before relieving him & starting one to one interaction with the students, I asked Bhatiya sir nervously one more time, "Will it really work effectively?"

"Sure son! It will." He said & smiled with an ease.

*

"THE MISSING PIECE. Doesn't it sound like something raw, something incomplete?" A boy, perhaps in the 5th or 6th row, asked.

"Lemme clear this confusion first. It is P-E-A-C-E, not P-I-E-C-E." I announced by spelling both the words separately.

"Anyways, your question still stands valid," I added while pointing towards the questioner. "The peace which has been missing in my life is because of a precious piece of friendship. So both these, piece & peace, are interconnected."

"Has writing this book, really come up with some aid?" Another question was thrown at me from the audience.

"Waiting for the right time to let things fall into place on their own wasn't working either. So I chose to write." I replied.

"What's your meaning of 'The missing peace'?" A girl with the spectacles stood up & asked.

"These 200 pages," I picked up the book which was kept over the table & replied.

The crowd responded in laughter.

"What's this book is all about? I mean its genre & what kind of readers did you to target?" Again a girl asked.

"I don't think I look like some intellectual with a vast experience of some 30 odd years." I tried to add a funny connotation and continued, "Rest assured, you'll easily relate the content of this book to yourself. It is all about friendship, love, life & much more."

"As an alumnus, what do you miss most about this college?" Siddhant aka Sid sitting with the GANG in the first row joined the rapid-fire team and asked mischievously this time.

"The privilege of being a student," I answered trying not to look at them.

Meanwhile, I picked up a water bottle from the table kept in front of us. While drinking, I looked at Bhatiya sir. He was busy with his cell phone, pressing a lot of keys at much speed with intensity. He was certainly texting someone, I guessed and put the bottle down.

"Putting a full stop to your technical career for writing a book doesn't sound practical. Don't you think it is risky?" someone from the back asked.

"Pretty much and I won't advise anyone to do the same. Anyways, I have already enrolled myself for a Master's Degree while the book was in the pipeline," I replied confidently as I was already prepared for that question.

"Vishesh, May I?" Our Dean, who was sitting in the front row, raised his hand & asked.

"No sir, not you. You'll definitely get into the technicality, like always." I replied with a wit.

He laughed. And the entire hall followed, seeing him laughing.

"Please! Please! Just one question," Dean said in his familiar Tamil accent.

"Sure sir, you are always allowed. Don't embarrass me by requesting." I tried to show some courtesy.

"According to the title and whatever you have revealed about this book till now, I can smell some sense of guilt in it. So how was the experience of writing it?" He asked in his quick accent.

"See sir, I already knew that you will ask the toughest question," I replied to lighten up the ambiance.

The crowd burst out into laughter.

"Actually it was a kind of *déjà vu*. I found myself in the same situation about which once I got to know through someone. And as he told me, it was some bizarre feeling of dissatisfaction while being satisfied already. I felt pity for him. And that was all I could do for him at that time because it was his feelings that were asking for more. But actually, I was able to sense his helplessness and anxiety. And the biggest irony was that the culprit himself was the victim too. He couldn't do much about it or I would like to correct myself by saying that, he was brave enough to live with the prejudiced half-truth, without complaining or explaining about it.

And without shying away from the fact, I accept that I don't possess such a quality like he does & I then, felt like it is high time to let the world know, along with him too, that why there can't be another KABEER BHAAGWAT, who himself doesn't know about his legends. And yes! Penning down this book again took me through the ups & downs of my past but also helped me a lot to recover from the pain of losing my two soul mates."

My voice crumbled while speaking the last few words. I got a tad emotional but in actuality, it was my pride which took over my voice. And, without any further ado, Bhatiya sir took over, sensing the fragility of the occasion. I slipped onto the couch and again picked up the bottle of water to drink while some random visuals of my past started flashing across my mind.

*

PARALLELLY,

Somewhere inside a room, a boy picked up an envelope placed on the table and opened it. He read it quickly and then kept looking for something in the bookshelf, some book, perhaps. Instead of looking one by one at each book, his eyes started wandering through the shelf from left to right and vice versa. It took him just two quick lookouts and his hunt was over. He dragged the book outwards with hastiness and kept tossing and turning its pages. The book was not in a good condition, though its pages were sort of okay. The boy literally tried to judge the book by its cover but alas! The book was coverless. He seemed a little bit confused and therefore again opened it randomly and after making few more such attempts, he found that it actually wasn't a book. It was a manuscript which had a lot of deletions and corrections done by ink, almost on every page. A raw content seemed enough to make him confused and excited altogether which finally made him decide to start from the very first page available on it. While throwing himself comfortably onto the bean bag placed opposite to the shelf, he started off.

****

CHAPTER 3

"MANNERISM"

**AUGUST 2007,**

**NEW DELHI**

"Don't try to move even an inch from here," our senior instructed us.

"You guys are brought here to cheer for us, so keep doing it without fail," another senior gave his share of directions.

I, along with my entire class, in the very first week of my college got that auspicious job of cheerleading for the senior batches, who were about to kick off their friendly football match. They were ready to commence _on_ the field and we were already being told to do our respective job _off_ the field. Still, we were jammy that they didn't bring us some pompom to dance with. It was no rocket science for me to understand within no time why engineering has been known to be the toughest course among all the other courses. They made us sit on the grass skirting the ground and unfortunately I got my seat in the very first row, because of which I also got to know (after spending some more time over there) that the match was played between the 3rd-year and 4th-year students.

As the whistle blew, the game started and we also started doing what we were brought to the field for. None of us exactly knew which team we were to support but each one of us was very well aware of the fact that we had to cheer continuously, no matter whichever team it was. It was literally like we were falling ass over teakettle. I was all but praying that I can go back to the classroom safely without being a helpless prey of so-assumed banned Ragging. I had heard a lot about it and now the possibilities were more of me shaking hands with it. It was some automatic self-generated feeling, which redirected me from doing my primary function of being called over there. I kept traveling continuously through my thought process with a blank face and bent head.

"Don't look up," a girlish voice came strongly from the row just behind me, in a warning tone.

Though my head was already bent, yet I checked it again using all my senses. The warning wasn't for me actually. A male voice answered her back, sitting behind me and unknowingly settled down my exponentially increasing restlessness.

"So if we can't put our heads up, then what's the motive of bringing us here? What are we? Some blind audience."

The boy replied to the girl sitting next to him and exactly behind me.

"Don't act smart. I think this is your first day in college and if you really don't want to get in a hot potato, follow what I just said," the girl whispered, yet it was audible to me too.

"Now don't sound like as if you have been staying here since your birth." The male voice retorted quickly.

I was listening to all that ramble of theirs and my intuition assured me that they would sooner get the reward for their million dollar debate. Unluckily, the very next moment, my personal gut feeling turned out true as a public show.

"Hey you two, what's cooking up there?" an angry male voice interrupted their one to one talk.

"Nothing sir," the girl responded with the lamest excuse as if everyone else was dumb.

The senior, the possessor of that angry voice was probably some extra player of the team, sitting there unwillingly, like us. His voice sounded extra-frustrated for some unknown reason. Well, seniors generally have that tendency of being rude to their juniors especially to the nascent batches and they deliberately look for them to spit out their shit on. Luckily for him, he got his opportunity too soon.

"Stand up you fools and come here. Don't you know any manners?" the angry senior shouted and kept continuing some more.

A chuckling sound came in response. The girl who replied to the previous question had already stepped over before letting the senior complete his set of criticisms and came forward. Perhaps it was the boy sitting beside her, who chuckled.

But really, 'Manners in Ragging' just sounds like 'Dishonesty needs Honesty' to survive. I found it hypothetical as well as hypocritical but more than that it was sarcastic, the other way around. Probably that chuckling boy would have the same opinion as mine and that was why he found humour in that angry bastard's sentence & hence chuckled.

"Do you need an invitation to come here?" the senior asked pointing out to someone, the same boy perhaps.

The boy immediately stood up and also stepped forward, learning from the girl's mistake.

"What's your name?" the Senior asked the boy.

"Kabeer," the boy replied.

"Full name and keep your eyes down at the second button from the top of your shirt. Don't you know how to give a proper introduction?" the angry senior threw a series of questions at Kabeer.

"Sir, he has joined today only. It's his first day in college." The girl replied for Kabeer. She must have lowered her eyes while answering, I guessed.

"So what, and who are you? His sister?" the angry senior tried to laugh for the first time in that entire session of who's who.

"No sir, I am Radhika Thapar, C.R, ECE 1st-year." The girl replied very politely for herself this time.

'What the hell is a C.R?' I thought to myself. I too was just 2 days old over there.

"Okay, you go and sit & you, Mr. First day, keep standing here," the Senior instructed as if he was briefing some secret strategy on how to attack the opposite team.

The boy with the name Kabeer, without any further resistance, obeyed the instruction thrown at him.

For some 30 odd minutes, the game continued but remained goal-less as none of the players scored any goal for their respective teams. Seniors decided to call the match off as some of the players had their classes to attend. So the match was over, resulting in a draw and which brought a sigh of relief for us. We, the cheerleaders were happy because the game had ended and it also ended the dominance of seniority over juniority, at least for the time being. I could finally go to the class to study for which I actually got admitted there and therefore along with rest of the cheerleaders, I too was waiting for the official permission from seniors to leave the field. Kabeer who was standing next to the seniors interfered with an unnecessary idea of penalty shoot-out for quickly deciding the certain result of the match. A few players disagreed and scolded him for his preaching and advice. I too cursed him for trying to extend our stay on the field under the supervision of those rude seniors. I was praying to God for the denial of his stupid proposal but perhaps God was not amused with my prayers at all. More heads, more minds, and therefore more suggestions, which finally led to the decision of going for a penalty shoot-out but with a new player to play as a goalkeeper for one of the teams, as per what I understood from their conversation. Kabeer was in a pickle, I could bet on it. Advisors run no risks and perhaps he didn't give it a second thought before speaking. He wasn't aware of the fact that his piece of advice would turn as a double-edged sword. But, it can't be undone now. He was option-less and probably clueless too.

Out of the blue, Kabeer came to me and asked to borrow my sports shoes humbly. My eyes were already lowered for the last one hour and therefore I was already looking at his shoes as he came towards me and stopped in front of me. He himself was wearing black coloured ankle length boots. I wanted to say no, but because of the presence of seniors, I couldn't refuse. He asked me again for them. This time I looked up at his face and that was the first time, I saw him. He was wearing a grey coloured T-shirt and cargo pants in camouflage print over his archetype lean body. Unlike some muscular guy, he had a body built more of an athlete. He was tall about 6 feet. I had no exact opinion about his body proportion but the way he had carried himself, was attractive. His oval-shaped face had an innocent smile on lips which could resist anyone from going against him. His brown coloured semi-straight hair placed perfectly over his head, were shining in the sunlight just like his fair complexioned face.

He was just like us, a normal human being but still not like us. He had something charismatic about him which was binding me to look at him continuously. I hitherto was unable to figure it out, but surely my other senses had sensed it in the best possible way. Of course, he was the live example of handsomeness. I mean he looked better than me and better than most of us but still, there was something more special to him than what was appearing on the outside.

"Stay right here. I'll be back in 5 minutes," Kabeer said while wearing my shoes.

"Take care of my shoes," is what I actually wanted to say but I settled with just an "okay".

I bought this new pair of NIKE shoes by saving my pocket money for 6 months. I spent 3000 bucks on those branded shoes so that I could flaunt my accessories in the college. But here, I was donating them to a stranger for ball kicking.

Almost all my classmates had left the ground, obviously with the permission of seniors as we had a class of applied maths to attend next. Kabeer and I, were the only ones remaining from our batch, on the ground. Kabeer chose it for himself as well as for me. Well, I never went easy with maths in my entire life but facing maths was too convenient and suited me right then, than to confronting seniors and that too, alone. Well, beggars can't be choosers. I had no option. But not to be the prey of seniors was totally dependent on me and hence I wore Kabeer's heavy military boots and chose to go away from the ground so that no senior (present on the ground) could trace me and made me his personal entertainer.

Also, I was not some die-hard admirer of sports. So the result of the match didn't matter to me as much as the safely retrieving of my branded NIKE shoes.

But right then, my own safety held higher priority than anything else to me. And it didn't continue to bother me as soon I saw Kabeer being elevated high on the shoulders of seniors. From the distance, I could clearly see them singing and dancing, which assured me that everything was fine, at least on Kabeer's part.

Kabeer directly came to me after he was done celebrating, with a smile on his face. I was standing outside the canteen, which was next to the ground so that I could be easily visible to him. I also smiled back while looking at my shoes which fitted perfectly on his feet. They seemed fine and therefore I also felt fine.

"Won?" I asked as someone had to commence the conversation.

"Thanks to your shoes," he chuckled.

I too laughed along with him.

'LAUGHTER IS THE BEST MEDICINE', they say, but not here at the college at least for the youngest batch of the college.

"Share that bloody piece of the joke with us too," an angular voice interrupted our light moments. The third person appeared suddenly from nowhere.

No need to guess that it was some senior and hence following the so-called MANNERISM, we stopped laughing and kept our eyes down. The campus was just like a jungle in terms of seniors and juniors. We juniors were the most lovable and weakest animals, surrounded by every kind of predators, whether they themselves were animals or homo-sapiens.

"Nothing sir, I was telling him about the match," Kabeer told the truth humbly but to a wrong person for time being.

SLAP!

Kabeer got the instant reward on his face for telling the truth.

"Bring them inside the canteen," another senior standing at the entrance of canteen, suggested.

*

"Who the fuck you think, you are? OLIVER KAHN!" that arrogant senior yelled at Kabeer while sitting on the table like a goon, as we entered inside the canteen.

I got scared, angry and silent. Too many emotions in a single moment but actually, I was helpless. Helpless also as in I was busy in figuring out whether OLIVER KAHN was a football player or some soothsayer. I really had a poor intelligence quotient.

"Laugh *na*! Why aren't both of you laughing now, LOSERS?" that bastard again yelled at us as if we were his slaves.

"Really, you yourself were on the losing side and now addressing them as losers." Someone retorted to that asshole while stepping inside the canteen.

SLAP!

Kabeer, in no time received another one.

Now the person behind us gave up on his patience, came forward and pushed that angry beast backward.

"Enough Jassi, either learn to accept failures or otherwise resign from playing." The saviour of our asses warned the short-tempered senior named as Jassi.

Until now, the only thing I was damn sure about that match was that Jassi was on the side opposite to Kabeer's winning team. But it was still doubtful to me that which senior team had won it as the match was played between the two senior-most batches. The person who pushed back Jassi couldn't be his junior but might be his batch-mate, who loved to admire sportsmanship in a game and remained unaffected of that winning or losing. There were possibilities. But I got strong feelings that he must be our final year senior. In that tense situation, I was applying permutations and combinations (which I otherwise was never able to understand during school) to find out who could be who.

"Sir how come you dishonour me for these bloody juniors?"Jassi yelled again, but this time at his senior.

My assumption was correct. The saviour was senior to Jassi too. And I got to realize that Jassi usually spoke in that tone only, quite natural to him- LOUD & AGGRESSIVE.

"We'll talk later, I think you'd better leave right now," the senior instructed him calmly.

"DADA, 3 cokes please and one to Jassi too," he said to canteen's owner.

"Thank you, sir," I anticipatively said to him.

"Here no sorry, no thanks, just obey the seniors blindly." He apprised me with the code of conduct from the self-made rule book of seniors.

Rule makers are someone who either make rules not applicable to them or can alter any rule at any period of time. Well, he might have been one of the victims of that Rule-policy as a junior, who now was taking all the privileges of it by surpassing his rank to a senior.

I again fell silent.

"1 conceded and 4 saved. Extraordinarily played champ! I am totally impressed. Would you like to play for the college team? By the way, I am IMAAN SAIFI, your super senior from the final year." He appreciated Kabeer and then introduced himself unfollowing the MANNERISM.

I understood the reason then, why Kabeer was held high by the seniors. As Imaan sir said, he was extraordinary on the field and obviously saving 4 goals was really a big deal and that too when people around you were in search of a silly opportunity to kick your butt anyhow. I realized Jassi was not wrong. After all, he had a legitimate reason to slap Kabeer.

"Sir, myself Kabeer Bhaagwat, ECE 1st year," Kabeer introduced himself without any delay irrespective of what he was asked.

I followed suit.

The way I spoke was enough for Imaan sir (well, for everyone), to understand where I originally belonged to. Generally, I used to take care of my Mother tongue influence desperately so that I do not sound odd among those localities but in stressful occasions like such, one automatically switches to his actual base. And without further ado, Imaan sir asked me the obvious question, "BHOJPURI?" imitating my Bhojpuri tone.

I just nodded my head in reply.

"Then sing a Bhojpuri song and show some killer moves too," He requested in a light mood.

"Well, you both can be normal and look up," he added further.

Kabeer looked at me mischievously. I looked at him for a while and then looked away. I thought he would be sad or insulted, for those two tight slaps but contrary to my notions, he was quite balanced. His eyes were shining as if nothing had happened to him a few moments earlier. His confident eyes made me feel more nervous. Imaan sir made him sit next to himself and they both were enjoying their coke. I, with my share of coke, was standing in front of them helplessly. To be honest, if that time, I was asked for 10 tight slaps on my face, I would have chosen it without giving a second thought, but alas! Nobody planned on a negotiation.

"LET'S START CHAMP! And some Manoj Tiwari track,

okay?" Imaan sir flaunted his awareness about Bhojpuri world and laughed.

*

"Don't tell about this to anyone, buddy. It could happen to anyone of us." I pleaded to Kabeer as soon as Imaan sir and other seniors left the canteen.

"Now don't get started in a typical Bollywood style, man. 'First walk into my shoes and blah-blah.' I've already walked in your branded NIKE shoes, though they were bit tight on me." He, at his sarcastically best, teased me and continued.

"By the way, you were amazing, man. You just nailed it," He laughed while trying to copy my dance steps, which were actually just some weird poses made by me.

I was totally embarrassed and I almost felt like I was held naked in public. Actually, I was scared more of the fact that people would tease me for the rest of my stay over here if they got wind of my splendid performance. I had always been very conscious with regards to my image or in another way, I was conscious about the criticism I would get if I didn't follow the conventional way. I realized that I had been following the same since my senses were active and that was why pretending appeared to me easier to accomplish as compared to being myself. And because of that, the notions of that singing and dancing were continuously nagging at me like a thorn about to pierce my skin anytime soon.

Lunch break was hardly 15 minutes away. So we decided to spend the rest of the time in canteen itself as we had already happened to skip our maths class. Meanwhile, Kabeer returned me my shoes with a gesture of gratitude, which had totally slipped out of my overthinking mind.

*

"Where were you in the last period?" Radhika questioned Kabeer as he entered in the class after recess.

"What business do you have with it?" Kabeer questioned her back, irritatingly.

"I am the Class Representative. Tyagi sir, our maths professor instructed me to take the attendance of his class as he didn't turn up to teach today, because of some urgent meeting with the Dean." Radhika supported her answer with every possible detail she could pass on to Kabeer.

"Okay, so mark my attendance too. Why are you asking unnecessary questions when nobody knows whether I was present or not in the class?" Kabeer replied reasonably.

"Very smart, but actually I know something else too, which nobody knows," Radhika said tauntingly.

"Obviously, you can have every trivial information of the class. After all, you are the C.R." Kabeer replied back without getting affected with her taunts.

"So how many....?" Radhika left her statement mid-way and chuckled.

"Well, you are the almighty C.R. I think you can find out that silly thing yourself. Let me give you a hint." Kabeer said pointing his finger towards me, taunting her as well as me.

I absolutely turned into a heeder to their conversation as Radhika had already interrogated me earlier about that class bunk and in the temptation of convincing her to mark me present in the attendance sheet I spewed everything that had happened in canteen excluding my unmatchable dancing and singing performance. I knew it could cost me heftily as chances were Kabeer could also reveal about my incident to the entire class, as revenge. Hence I was listening to their argument oriented conversation with all my concentration. But as promised, Kabeer didn't say a word against me. Actually, he never promised me but I didn't know why had I expected it from him. The reason was unknown to me, but unknowingly, he had lived up to my expectations.

I decided to go to Kabeer's desk and asked to seek forgiveness as soon as Radhika was done with her million dollar interrogation.

"I am sorry bro, for all the nonsense. I felt, she would mark, both of our attendance as she asked me very politely regarding our absence. That's why I told her about that incident. I am really sorry bro. I didn't want to screw up the things intentionally." I tried to defend myself with lame excuses.

"It's okay." He replied in just two words for my too-long sorry speech as if he didn't care at all.

"And thanks for not telling about my shit." I patted his back for being my secret holder and moved back to my seat as the professor entered in the classroom.

****

CHAPTER 4

"COMPLAINT AND THE COWARD"

_"4 saves, not bad," Radhika tried to compliment Kabeer.

"What does 'not bad' mean? Complimenting me or kicking me?" Kabeer replied with his wit.

"Actually, I was trying to compliment your kicking." Radhika defended herself with an attacking humour.

"Well, for your information, I played as a goalkeeper and conceded just 1 goal." Kabeer apprised her with the fact of the matter.

We were performing some V-I characteristics of Zener-diode in the electronics laboratory. Radhika and I, were in the same group, sitting next to each other. I was trying to look immensely involved in performing the practical but actually, it was like rocket science for me to understand what and how to perform the respective practical. I held the black and red wires of the practical apparatus in order to look busy, but actually, I was interested more in listening to Radhika and Kabeer's conversation as they were just mind-blowing with their humour shots.

"Conceded 1 or 3," Radhika continued and was dominating in that sarcastic conversation.

"Oh, but by that calculation as well, I managed to win finally." Kabeer defended himself very neatly.

"I am sorry for yesterday. I shouldn't have asked you that stupid question. I already got to know about the incident through Vishesh." Radhika confessed, including me too in her confession note.

As I heard my name in that conversation that was supposed to be full of humour, I reacted as if I was thoroughly involved in doing my bit as a uber-studious kid and hence wasn't aware of my immediate surrounding activities.

"I wasn't offended at all neither by you nor by those slaps." Kabeer clarified and reduced Radhika's guilt.

"Are you sure?" She confirmed.

"Totally," He remained stuck to his words.

'What is happening man?' I thought in my head. A girl, beautiful as hell, was putting her ego aside and apologizing to a boy-next-door, for no reason and assuring the same again and the boy was reacting as if this was absolutely normal. He showed no sign of excitement, neither on his face nor in his speech. Was he really trying to play dumb or if he actually was? I swear if this had happened to me, I would have planned my family with that girl. But sadly, it wasn't happening with me.

Kabeer didn't bother to ask her anything else, neither logical nor stupid. He didn't even try to continue the conversation formally, unlike typical boys who get ready to offer their entire life to a girl, if she just asks for lending a pen. I also tried to read Radhika's reactions, but then she also didn't show any interest in an almost one-way-conversation with Kabeer further and got completely immersed in finding the V-I characteristics of Zener-diode.

*

Unlike Kabeer, it took me time to get over that canteen incident. Either I was emotionally offended or I had just overvalued that incident. But, one thing I was assured of was that I believed, Kabeer wouldn't tell anyone about it anytime. I wanted to remind him at a regular interval, to not speak about it, but he didn't show any such interest in being more-than-acquaintances with me & hence eventually I had to give up on my plan of being his reminder. I personally wanted to interact with him more, just more than those HI-HELLOS which we used to exchange as a gesture of greeting as we caught each other in the morning. I had passed more than half a month in college since my arrival, but I wasn't able to be friends with anyone in particular. I was not good at making friends. I wasn't gutsy enough to trust anyone just like that and I wasn't some cool dude either with whom people would like to be friends with. On the contrary, Kabeer had got all the genes to be a perfect and natural charmer. I was impacted by him to a great extent like others but at the same time, I didn't want to establish myself as a nagger to him. Neither my branded NIKE shoes nor my mind boggling dance was able to impress him in the first go and hence I indirectly tried to get into his life. I started reading his daily basic activities, but what I found was that he had no particular pattern. Basically, he was a happy go lucky person who had no regular friends, but someone would always be his constant companion.

Meanwhile, with passing time, I didn't see Radhika and Kabeer interacting with each other again nevertheless he was seen helping other female students of our class in their studies and other co-curricular activities every now and then. He used to keep a certain distance between himself and Radhika for some strange reason. In fact, he used to avoid her deliberately, is what I personally felt.

Anyways, Radhika and I had become friends by then, not the best ones but still more than just acquaintances and all credit went to those group activities.

*

"Let's go to the canteen, I am hungry," Radhika insisted to me.

We were sitting idle in the electronics laboratory as we had completed our nominated practical work faster than others, obviously only because of Radhika. As the lab attendant was busy in attending other groups who were still performing their practical, it was very easy for us to sneak away. I wanted to warn her about seniors who could possibly be present over there, but then I didn't. I didn't want to be perceived as dastardly, at least to her. As Radhika was the only girl in our 'practical group', so advising her to go with some other girl was not possible, as all others were busy in their respective share of work. Also, I was not so dumb either, to suggest her to go with some other boy.

"*Bhaiyya* 3 samosas," Radhika said to the minion working in the canteen as soon as we reached there.

"Make them 4, I'll also have 2," I corrected her.

"Dumbo, I'll eat 1 only." She reacted quickly and avowed me dumb.

"I thought you were really hungry.' I reminded her.

"Yeah I am, but 1 will do the job." She chuckled.

I was completely confused. Only for 1 samosa, she took that much risk! I really wanted to tell her that it wasn't funny at all and how funny it would become if we fell in the radar of some wrongheaded senior.

"Give them 2 energy drinks too, DADA! I'll pay the bill." Someone tried to oblige us.

Within a few days at college, I had understood very clearly that nothing was for free. That free service would cost us something hefty. Think of the devil and the devil had appeared. We instantly followed all the mannerism.

"You rocked the stage, the other day. Imaan sir told me. Is it true?" the free service provider asked something so personal which I didn't want to tell even myself.

"I am asking you, bastard." He yelled at me as I was nonresponsive.

I knew he was asking me. But after that pseudo-compliment, I went in a state of bewilderedness. His loud tone reminded me of someone known. Given a tad stress to my mind and it came up with a correct answer, he was Jassi. And I was in a pickle, I realized.

"Sorry sir," I reacted in those two words only.

"Why are you apologizing, my boy? Just bless us with some of your funky moves." Jassi requested in a no-requesting tone.

 His gang burst out in laughter as he roasted me.

"Sir, we need to go." Radhika disrupted them.

"Sure, but after the dance performance," Jassi finished his terms and conditions in no time.

"Sir we have a class to attend." I hollowly put an effort to save us.

"Don't argue with me, be quick and then you guys can go." He reacted as if he was the governing authority.

The way he tried to dominate us, eventually broke the patience of Radhika. She stood up angrily, held my hand tightly and without caring about the meaningless mannerism, warned them, "let us go, otherwise I am going to complain against you all." already befuddled, I was unable to react.

Any argument whether logical or not, by a junior is

enough to hurt the ego of seniority. And that confrontation was with Jassi, who hitherto would have felt that he was literally abused by us. To him, limits had been crossed and now it was his turn to make the score even. He was totally out of control as he lost his patience and in rage, he tried to tug Radhika's other hand so that she wouldn't be able to hold my hand anymore.

Radhika narrowly escaped an accident as she lost her balance with that sudden pulling of hand and was about to fall on the floor, but as she was already holding my hand tightly, it somehow helped her in not getting any possible injury.

Everyone was taken aback.

A complete silence took over the canteen.

*

"Call that boy too," Dean instructed to the peon Bittu.

Radhika, Jassi and I were already in the Dean's office. Radhika hadn't given Jassi a hoax call, he realized it very soon.

Jassi was completely helpless as the Dean got acquainted with everything through Radhika, exactly as the way things occurred plus she added Kabeer's slap incident too to make the complaint stronger (En route Dean's office, I told her that Jassi was the same guy who slapped Kabeer). We left no stone unturned in adding a full bag of salt to the Jassi's injuries.

The Dean, for his satisfaction wanted to confirm the

same from Kabeer & hence he was invited to join the party. Meanwhile, I was killing my time by observing the Dean's office with oblique sight. Well, that was my first time at his office. With some medals, trophies and other souvenirs, my eyes didn't find anything catchy apart from the elegant furniture. In fact, furniture reminded me of Jassi who was almost standing like a snag. I tried to read his facial expression with squinted eyes to my left, where he was standing. He was all sweaty, looking very nervous and deplorable, just opposite to what I had seen of him before.

Radhika standing to the extreme left of me was looking totally opposite to him, angry, confident and ruthless.

Kabeer arrived very soon. He was clueless, completely. Anyways, he asked for permission to join the party by greeting "Good afternoon" to the Dean.

The Dean greeted back in his Tamil accent. "Good afternoon son, come in. Kabeer Bhaagwat, right?" he confirmed.

Kabeer nodded his head in reply and entered with a bit of a hesitation. The Dean directly got to business, without any further preluding.

"Kabeer, how well do you know them?" Dean asked while pointing out at three of us.

"They are my classmates," Kabeer replied signaling towards us. "And he is our senior." He completed the verification process by pointing towards Jassi.

"Means you know him quite well?" Dean wrapped up.

"Not that much sir. We are just acquaintances. He once asked me for my introduction at the canteen, around 2-3 days ago." Kabeer spoke as he seemed already prepared for such kind of interrogation.

"Anything else, he did to you?" Dean tried on.

"No, sir. Yes, he offered me and Vishesh, each a coke as we finished our introduction." Kabeer lied looking at me.

"Are you sure?" Dean confirmed for the last time.

"Yes sir," He replied confidently.

"Okay, three of you, Go to your class and pay attention to your studies. This is your first year and I don't want you to indulge in any sort of nonsense. And directly report to me, if anyone tries to bully you inside or outside the campus (while looking at Jassi). One more thing, spend more time at classes than the canteen." Dean briefed us, the first year students.

The three of us obeyed him while Jassi was instructed to pause for a while.

"Coward," Radhika whispered as we were coming out of the interrogation room.

Kabeer was leading us, followed by me and then Radhika. I felt, it was loud enough to fall in his ears but he didn't react at all. Not sure if he actually didn't hear it or deliberately acted like that. None of us uttered a single word thereafter, en-route the classroom.

****

CHAPTER 5

"THE BRO CODE"

The complaint could go in any which way, I knew it very clearly. But I was sure that the verdict wouldn't come in our favour, precisely mine and not officially but yes illegally. And complaining because of a girl was completely a different issue altogether. I was in the classroom and brooding over what was going to happen next, as a voice interrupted my thought process. A senior most probably of 2nd year, came at the doorstep of our classroom, looking for me. "Imaan sir is calling you in the hostel," he announced from the doorstep itself as I had already stood up when he took my name. I had gotten familiar with and recognized all the students by the time, as there were not so many students in the college due to limited courses offered and also their body language used to say it all. In fact, generally, those 'seniors of higher levels' used to send the 'seniors of basic level' as their ambassadors in such sort of circumstances. The invitation was expected and my presence was mandatory. The more time I would've taken, the more restlessness would've grown inside me. And as it was our free period, so without any delay I decided to go along with him.

While passing through the aisle of the classroom, I looked at Kabeer as I passed by him. He himself was looking at me. I was shivering while sweating bullets. He noticed it. The upcoming few minutes in my life would be the toughest moments of my life at that college, I sensed it soon. And I was all alone.

That senior who was taking me to the HELL was thinking of himself as a super cop who had literally nailed the opportunity of grabbing the most wanted dacoit of some wilderness. He preached a few things to me and we kept heading towards the destination he was told to. Well, it wasn't *his* post-mortem before the funeral. He did his share of work effectively and in couples of minutes, we were standing outside the door of room no. 69 in the hostel, when we finally stopped walking. I was told to enter the room and the boy who brought me there regressed from the door itself.

There were two persons sitting on two different beds placed at the two far corners of the room. As I entered there, I was instructed to sit on the chair placed beside me. Thereafter, I was told to look up, which I did on the second go as they insisted. Imaan sir and Jassi were those two persons, present in the room excluding me.

"So you love filing complaints?" Imaan sir initiated as I put my head up.

I responded with silence.

"Pass him down the letter." He instructed to Jassi.

Jassi silently got up from his bed and handed me a folded piece of paper, without looking at me.

I opened it and read it murmuringly.

WARNING LETTER, written at the center top of it in BOLD.

TO,

Mr. JASVINDER SINGH

Jassi was actually Jasvinder Singh, as revealed by that really important piece of paper. So I discovered something interesting which had eventually given me an opportunity to have a direct word with Kabeer. He would surely pat my back for this out of the box discovery, I just thought. Before I could move to read the further content of the letter, Imaan sir interrupted me in the middle with a question.

"What do you actually want to be, Vishesh?" he asked politely.

"An engineer," I thought twice before speaking.

"Really, are you sure?" he tried to confirm from me.

"Yes sir," I said hesitatingly.

"So why the hell are you trying to be a hero?" Imaan sir yelled in sheer rage.

I fell silent. He did not. His eyes staring at me were enough to make me understand that he was offended personally.

"Just because of a silly girl," He said being more concerned this time.

"No sir," I said and shook my head.

"Really, then why didn't you lodge a complaint by yourself when I forcefully made you dance? Answer me, you knucklehead." He stood up and shouted.

Jassi, who again found solace in his bed, was sitting quietly. He was as reaction less as a dead body.

"Don't you have anything more to say, moron? You think you have become some revolutionary. Now I am giving you a chance to prove yourself a hero. Go and complain to Dean about me." He kept coming closer to me while speaking.

He pulled me vertically above the chair by tugging at my shirt's collar with both his hands as soon as I became reachable to him. I got scared and started shivering again. I wasn't sure if he would slap me or not, but definitely, the next step would have been pushing me back onto the surface. In anticipation I prepared myself for the jerk I was about to receive but before the execution of any possible action, somebody reached the doorstep. The upcoming action and its reaction received a pause command due to the sudden pop up of an unacknowledged interruption. Imaan sir immediately turned his head almost 180 degrees to look at the door. I too looked in the same direction without requiring that much effort as the door was directly in my line of sight. It was Kabeer. He was panting badly.

"Sorry sir," He quickly reacted and asked for permission to enter the room.

"Come bro." The reaction-less Jassi replied this time very politely, coming back to consciousness.

A warning letter changed both, tone and language of Jassi, too fast and too easily.

"Thanks, sir. Please leave him, sir. Let me apprise you with the complete truth." Kabeer said catching his breath as if he was going to unveil some much-awaited secret on a murder mystery.

He further took a pause to catch his breath completely and then continued, "Vishesh didn't act to cause any fault, sir. He had no intentions to file a complaint against Jassi sir. He went with Radhika only to accompany her because they both are good friends, nothing else. And before going to Dean's office, he came to me and told everything, that's why when Dean asked me regarding that slap case, I simply denied. You can ask Jassi sir about it."

Kabeer stated his self-cooked story which I guess he thought of, while sprinting towards the hostel. Meanwhile, Imaan sir restored his cool and let me loose.

"Jassi has already told me about it, champ." Imaan sir replied calmly using his catchphrase 'CHAMP', which meant he had believed what Kabeer said.

"I am offended not because of that complaint, but by the medium he chose to go to file it." Imaan sir justified his logic of getting infuriated while putting his arm around Kabeer's shoulder.

"Yes sir but he was option-less at that time. He shied away from refusing her also. You know that girl thing." Kabeer tried to explain my situation which was somehow true in a way.

"That's my point, the girl thing and that's why I am worried. Make him understand about it too." Imaan sir advised Kabeer to advise me.

"And you, Mr. Hero, try to use your mind too." I then got my share of advice directly from him too.

I personally said sorry to both of them and came out of the room with Kabeer, as we were permitted to leave the room. While passing through the stairs of the hostel, we kept our head bent. We were almost running on the stairs, trying to leave the hostel premises as soon as possible. I was crying continuously since after I left the room. Kabeer noticed it later when we reached the ground level. I myself was not sure of the exact reason why my tears chose to fall off my eyes automatically? The reason was absent. I came out of the room without any harm but I could have been harmed, perhaps that was why I felt so. Kabeer consoled me patting my back, "It's all okay dude, don't cry. Everything is fine now."

"I am sorry Kabeer. I really am." I held his hand tight.

I didn't know how many times I had uttered the word 'SORRY' since my arrival in that college, which happened hardly about 20 days ago. But this time, I meant it, completely from the core of my heart to someone who emerged as my saviour, risking himself without any reason.

"Why did you risk yourself for me?" I spoke my mind, wiping out tears off my face.

"To save you," He replied with the easiest answer.

"But why buddy?" I insisted.

"I felt like I could save you, that's why only. But I lied over there and all, and maybe you don't second my thought but what to do, you were option less. And yes, complaining about wrong is your right and tolerating oppression is itself a sin, but filing complaint is also not the complete solution. I am not trying to discourage you but this world doesn't run completely on the principle of 'LIVE AND LET OTHERS LIVE'. Try to be on the safe or less affected side first." Kabeer answered my question with some real pieces of advice.

"I didn't get you completely." I honestly remarked.

He smiled. He smiled like a baby, all from his heart. He simply did what he felt like doing but perhaps he didn't know that what it meant to me. He could also get punished for deliberately interfering into the matter but he still took a risk for me. Maybe he thought of doing it because Imaan sir was involved in it and therefore he had seen a bit of a possibility to convince his 'already impressed mind with Kabeer' with his fool-proof story. But the bottom line was, he risked his ass, no matter if it was a calculated risk or not. But then his innocent smile revealed it all that he wasn't available there to prove his heroics. It was something else, something bigger than that, compassion perhaps. He really sensed my nervousness and anxiety when I was leaving the classroom. He realized my helplessness towards me and towards the situational crisis. I was option-less but I had to face the repercussions of what had already been done. And yes, that was his unique trait which made him look so lustrous and which I was unable to reckon when I saw him for the first time. Aura is the accurate term to define that sensation around him what my other senses had sensed in the first go but my mind was unable to describe at that time. His smile had the transparency of his genuineness. He smiled all from his heart and that was something I was touched especially with. His heroics, his intelligence, and his innocence altogether made me emotional. And then when he smiled with utmost simplicity, I was moved to tears again. He himself hugged me sensing my emotions. Kinship was all I felt strongly with him.

*

Kabeer and I had almost reached to the campus gate as I saw Radhika sitting in the lawn area, which was right next to the main passage on which we were walking. Radhika sitting on a bench was looking like she was eagerly waiting for someone.

I looked at my watch. It was almost 1-hour post leaving time. Radhika came towards us, as she saw us.

"Hey still here, waiting for someone?" I asked from the distance.

She lived in a rented apartment outside the campus away from her family like me, Kabeer and many others.

Before coming here, she was living with her family in their native place, somewhere in between the border of Punjab & Himachal Pradesh where she lost all of them in a village riot at a very tender age. As she was alone, left from her family, her maternal uncle, who himself was childless, adopted and took her with them. She was brought up by her maternal aunt and uncle and therefore with their unconditional love and destined life, she found her parents in them and hence started addressing them as her mother and father.

She once told me how her mother i.e. maternal aunt, insisted to come with her, when she took admission over here in college and how melodramatically Radhika refused her to come. Her mother cried a lot when she finally left the village to join college. And here, she was residing in a girl's Paying Guest (PG) facilty, located near the campus with roommates not from our college.

Our campus was situated at the Delhi Faridabad border, way far from Delhi. The college used to offer hostel facility only to the boys but it had very limited seats, so the only but reasonable option was to stay as a P.G. or rent a room nearby for people like us. I had also rented a 1 BHK flat in Saket, sharing it with 2 other friends of mine, who also belonged to my village and were working in Delhi. Thanks to Delhi Transport Corporation for its frequent bus services on that particular route, because of which I could rely on Buses as a fast and convenient mode of transportation for me to travel on my way to college back and forth as it was barely 10kms away from my place of residence. I wasn't aware much about

Kabeer's stamping ground till then, though I knew he was a day scholar only.

Anyway, looking at Radhika coming towards us, I stopped while Kabeer continued walking, alone. He didn't bother to look back even for once and stepped out of the Campus gate in no time. I wanted him to stop and stay but, because of some certain possibility of awkwardness, I didn't try to stop him.

"What was he doing with you, fake consolation or something?" Radhika being judgemental commented about Kabeer.

"No actually he..." I was confused from where to start as she herself interrupted me in the middle.

"Let's leave him. Did you cry? Did they beat you?" Radhika asked quickly as she looked at my face.

"Nope that's how I naturally look," I said mealy-mouthed.

"Shut up." She smiled.

"Why? Do you want to again complain against them?" I poorly tried to crack a joke.

"Very funny, let's go. I am already late." Radhika said.

As her P.G. home wasn't very far, just walking distance from campus, after walking some 50 odd steps together, we separated and took our respective paths.

I went to the bus stop, waited for a while and then took the bus to my destination, Saket.

****

CHAPTER 6

"THE 'F' FACTOR"

Time was not passing all too soon for me in the first semester. But befriended by Kabeer and Radhika helped me amply in not analysing the pace of time. I was friends with both of them, but they both were not so with each other. Kabeer's carefree attitude and first few impressions on Radhika were the main reason behind their 'NO-TALK-EXPEDITION'.

Well, I had already told her about how Kabeer risked his ass to save mine from the seniors who were really upset because of that complaint we filed against them. I thought she would be glad to know the secret behind my unharmed and successful settlement of matter but contrary to that she scolded me and criticized the way, Kabeer handled the matter.

Radhika was a self-made girl, who was very well aware of her fundamental rights. She was very gutsy and all the credit went to her upbringing. The way she did things had the sheer glimpse of the way she had been brought up. She always preferred and expected things in a very systematic way. She was forthright and hence loved to do everything in the same manner. That was why she didn't seem impressed with Kabeer's exaggerated heroic effort.

Whereas, Kabeer's idea of leading life was, 'LIVE AND LET OTHERS LIVE'. Not that he always followed it exactly but he did a good attempt of it most of the times. Or in a better and my original set of words, I would like to define his ideology as 'RISE HIGH AND RAISE HIGH'. He was an absolute genius but not over-ambitious. He loved to live a hassle-free life. His biggest asset was his cool composure. At situations where most of us panicked, he would come up with a working plan. His oratory had something magical in it. He was so tactful that he could inject his own idea in one's mind very easily. He had a broader vision of life. He was influential. That was why he managed to convince Imaan sir with ease with his fake story over me.

The constant company of Radhika and Kabeer was making me a better person altogether. Radhika's zest for correcting things and Kabeer's vision of seeing the other side of everything were unknowingly shaping up my colourful future. But no greatness can be achieved overnight. It takes a tad more than everything one is committed for.

And my improved version was thousands of miles away from my then 'me'.

*

Our second semester had already commenced and the emphasis of ragging was getting dull as compared to earlier. Actually, we got so accustomed to it that it became a part and parcel of our college life and therefore started appearing less-affective later on.

The new semester brought a sigh of relief from the familiar ghost of ragging, but a new problem was about to knock at our door or precisely only at my door.

RUMORS SPREAD LIKE WILDFIRE IN THE JUNGLE.

We were sitting idle in the classroom after recess, killing our time doing nothing and waiting for the professor to arrive. Somebody in the first row had started rumours that the head of the department was coming with the 1st-semester result. The news of the results petrified me completely. This news might be a hoax, I tried to be optimistic and tried consoling myself falsely but deep down inside, I already knew the truth of my poor performance in the examinations. The notion of getting exposed to public in the next few minutes had me totally drenched in sweat even in the month of February.

The wait was finally over and all rumours came to an end when the H.O.D arrived in a minute or two with a printed sheet of paper in his hand. Without wasting a single second, he introduced himself to the class. Professor Ramesh Bhatiya, the H.O.D used to teach the final year students usually and this was his short visit to our class just to announce the result. He, in his unique style initiated that was really different from the other professors I had seen until then.

"Dear students, your 1ˢᵗ-semester results are out and as this is your first result, following the traditions of our college I am here only to announce the name of the best 3 performing students of this last semester along with their percentages respectively.

Before that, I am glad to say that around 80% students of this batch have passed the 1ˢᵗ semester. You will be happy to hear that this is the finest result among all 1ˢᵗ year batches in the history of this college. Congratulations to all of you for being the best in the business. And those who have not been able to pass the examinations should need to improve them, learning from their fellow students.

Now its time to announce the big names and here is the list;-

- Radhika Thapar at 3ʳᵈ position with 76.8%

 - Lucky Joshi at 2ⁿᵈ position with 78.9%"

The H.O.D took a pause just to create a panicking anticipation in the students very like the anchor of a reality show. I was miles away from such feelings as I already knew I wasn't in that race but still I was curious enough to know the name. He continued after taking his time.

"Who could be the topper of the batch, any guesses?" the H.O.D asked and run his eyes from left to right towards the class. "Okay without any further ado let me announce the name, and the name is Kabeer Bhaagwat with 84.3%!"

"A huge round of applause for all three of them!" H.O.D ended his announcement on a requesting note and he himself started clapping followed by others.

Everybody including me got dumbstruck by the latest announcement, I guess. Yes, we all knew Kabeer was spontaneous and good at studies but nobody was expecting him to emerge as the topper of the batch. For a moment, I forgot my pain of possibly not clearing the examination (though I hadn't seen my results yet I was sure that faculty couldn't cause any blunder).

I, as usual, was in the state of bewilderedness like every time, as I receive something other than regular expectations. Still, I was conscious enough to sense whatsoever happening around in the surrounding.

Lucky went directly to congratulate Kabeer as the H.O.D left the room, but his expressions actually were not supporting his words. Lucky had become our dear friend by then, but habitually he was very competitive and concerned about the number game and perhaps that was the reason for his languid wishes. Like Kabeer, he was also an all-rounder, a better one but not the best. At least results had proved him the second best.

But our third best seemed quite content with the result, one couldn't say exactly what, but her face wasn't showing any expression of regression or envy. As an epitome of a lady, she went to congratulate Lucky, who had just returned back to his seat with despair on his face.

As the H.O.D who had already left the class, after announcing the result and gave us a period break to celebrate as a reward, the entire class had started making most of that opportunity. While other students were busy with their celebrations and felicitations, I checked my result on that printed sheet which the H.O.D had left on the table, before leaving the classroom.

ROLL NO. 2744573 - VISHESH PRATAP SINGH   (F)

That 'F' alphabet written against my name was suitably applicable to me either which way I could reckon. I checked out the details. Failed in applied physics and applied maths, to be precise.

So I was unable to secure even passing marks in those two subjects. In fact, I was expecting F in Basic electronics as well and hence I checked the details again in order to find if it was correct or some printing mistake. Failed in two subjects was mentioned in the details and therefore my expectation was really wrong and by that calculation, my result was way better than what I had actually hoped for.

Kabeer and Radhika both came to me as I returned back to my seat after checking my result which didn't need to be checked, actually. Like good friends, they started consoling me over my less than ordinary performance but ended up in congratulating each other for their extraordinary performances and as usual, Radhika accelerated the initiation revealing her goodness one more time.

"Congratulations Kabeer for emerging as a dark horse." She congratulated him along with a compliment.

"Thanks, Radhika but this dark horse or underdog is just people's opinion or I would rather like to address those people as inexperienced judges," Kabeer said correcting Radhika's complementing statement.

"Yeah seriously, your result proved them so." She replied stamping her agreement on his statement.

Kabeer smiled.

"Well, you can congratulate me too. Not as good as you but still managed to be in the top 3." She reminded him of her performance too.

"Oh! I am... I am so sorry, I was about to congratulate you. Many Congratulations to you by the way." Kabeer said admitting his mistake.

"No issue at all, at least I am happy to know that you also use the word 'sorry'." She taunted.

"When I genuinely feel that my act is a mistake, only then." He said applying his terms and conditions and chuckled.

I thought it would just be a casual congratulatory meet like their earlier general 'Hi-Hellos' but the way they were interacting, revealed that they both were in a mood for a patch-up. I was already frustrated because of my results and their 'without-notice-patch-up' meeting over my desk, was rubbing salt to my wounds as I really wanted sympathy for myself that time from them and they were behaving as if they were the only two humans left in this universe.

"So don't you feel you should've said sorry to me for hiding the actual incident from the Dean and proving my allegations just unreal," Radhika tried to question Kabeer's 'genuine mistake' meaning.

"Well, what else can you expect from a 'COWARD'?" Kabeer questioned back instantly.

Like Radhika, I too wasn't sure that if he had really heard the word 'coward' that day but right then his question put our unsure assumption to a definite end. It was a total shock for both of us as it came against our perception at an unexpected point of time. Well, shock does mean that. I looked at Radhika, who was already looking at me totally dumbfounded.

"Can you guys please find some other place to chit-chat?" I tried to swerve the face of the conversation.

Radhika was dead silent. She had no other option either but I could act as a panacea for that awkward moment that occurred and I nailed the opportunity by throwing my emotional bomb at them. The only profitable thing I got of not passing the semester, served as a tool to make Kabeer phlegmatic over the 'coward' discussion.

"Sorry bro, really sorry," Kabeer apologized quickly for getting carried away.

"Sorry Vishesh," Radhika too apologized by the same token.

"Kabeer, I would like to tell you something, only if you allow me to. Can I have a few minutes from your valuable time?" Radhika requested in a very professional way.

Girls always do complete justice to mannerism whether

it's speaking, eating or anything else. They are quite ideal that way, I realized.

Kabeer accepted her request without throwing any tantrums at her and took her to his seat, which was two seats ahead of mine, in the same column.

By then the class got almost vacant as nearly most of the students went outside the classroom. Only 4-5 students were there excluding the three of us. So it didn't need me to turn into a heeder (as I had become one, a few times earlier) in order to hear the Kabeer-Radhika's secret conversation which actually wasn't so much of a secret after all as they were audible quite well.

"I am sorry for that again," Radhika said while making herself comfortable on the seat.

"Actually you need not be. You did what you felt like that particular moment and I did what I felt right." Kabeer made the equation easy.

"You know, that Jassi tried to interact by contacting me through phone even before that complaint scenario. I don't know how he got my number." She told to Kabeer.

"Any particular reason of contacting," He investigated.

"He proposed to me *yaar*. I clearly refused that time itself and also warned to file a complaint against him." She said in despair.

"Over the phone itself?" He asked funnily as if filing complaint was her only hobby.

"And then in the canteen, when he tried to bully Vishesh, I really lost my cool. That was why I decided to complain and also added your incident in it, without asking you. I just wanted to make the complaint stronger, nothing else, I swear." She added totally ignoring Kabeer's jab at humour.

"Okay, has he tried to contact you again anytime?" He further investigated.

"Nope, not as such," she replied after recalling something.

So that was the reason behind Jassi's changed behavior and droopy-droopy look in the hostel. Well, he lost his chance to woo Radhika after all. I thought in my head.

"I was actually offended by seeing that you tried to save Jassi, who never misses an opportunity to bully any junior, he meets. Nonetheless, it was personal more, I totally accept it but your true statement could have been very helpful for us." She explained why she was upset with him.

"Radhika, every person has a different way of doing things. You cannot handle everyone by being you every time. Sometimes you need to transform yourself like them or sometimes just opposite to them, to cut the deal and that transformation purely shows the versatility of being you. Not every time but most of the times, it works. And moreover, I didn't want to make it an issue in the long run. It would have given us more trouble for no reason. We are here to study, not to make war." Kabeer justified his vision.

"And now that you have started the topic of Jassi then I think I should also tell you that he had tried to threaten me multiple numbers of times and the reason was you," Kabeer dropped a new bomb.

"What? *Me*? How come?" She asked surprisingly emphasizing more on 'me'.

"He might've felt that there is a thing going between you and me as some of his sycophants told him about our interactions. Also, I didn't want you to get into crunches because of me, that's why I reduced talking to you or you may even say I started ignoring you." Kabeer explained everything at length.

"Stupid! Couldn't you tell me even once?" Radhika scolded him.

"So that you could have filed another complaint against him," He chuckled.

"Shut up!" She said and smiled seeing him smiling.

"Well, when I actually feel I am capable alone, I don't shy away taking one for the team." He said and winked at Radhika.

"You are crazy." She adored him.

"Well, right now this 'crazy' is the topper." He replied again with a smile.

"So where is my treat?" she asked more with kinship.

"Anytime," He approved her.

"Anywhere?" she asked to confirm.

"Wherever you say," He became more generous.

"Okay, I'll let you know tomorrow." She continued.

"Tomorrow is Sunday, college off." He replied back.

"So give me your number, I'll tell you over the phone," she tried to make most of the situation and acted faster than the speed of light.

Radhika fed his number in her cell phone and was waiting for some response from him but he didn't ask anything further, particularly for her number. I was never able to figure it out anytime that whether it was deliberate or natural with him but he always used to do that. He had a tendency to make people fall for him first and then leave them in the lurch, by pretending himself completely innocent and a newbie. Nevertheless, that was the least of Radhika's problem as she had already taken a giant leap forward in her friendship with Kabeer. The 'F' factor had finally come into the picture then as friendship for them and failure for me.

****

CHAPTER 7

"SAVE THE PRINCESS"

"Hello!" Kabeer replied from the other side of the call.

"Hi Kabeer, it's me Radhika." Radhika introduced herself to Kabeer.

"Oh! Hello, Radhika. I thought you just love to collect numbers but you do call on those numbers. Quite impressive, I must say." He started the conversation in a light mood.

"At least I have yours, but you didn't even bother to ask for mine." Radhika back talked him.

"Anyway, how are you? Everything okay at your side?" She asked politely after a while.

"Yes of course! By the way, why did you doubt my wellness?" He asked.

"Really, you want me to answer this. Don't pretend, okay!" She replied sounding very upset.

Kabeer sensed it immediately.

"Sorry madam for not turning up to the fresher's party." He directly came to the point and apologized for it.

Yes, it was our fresher's party, few hours before Radhika and Kabeer's phone call. She probably didn't find any appropriate reason to make a call to him any sooner, after getting his number. Probably, Kabeer's unconventional attitude of not asking for her number put her in some sort of confusion but today she couldn't stop herself from calling him. And it was quite obvious as he didn't attend the fresher's party. The one, who was perceived as the most eligible student in the youngest batch of the college, had skipped the big day.

The reason was untold. But his absence became a blessing in disguise for Lucky as he was adjudged as Mr. Fresher after Kabeer didn't turn up to the event without any prior info.

"And obviously, you are not going to reveal the reason," Radhika taunted Kabeer.

"What should I tell you? There is no such particular reason. I just didn't feel like coming over there." He added a lame excuse.

"Really, everyone was asking for you, even seniors kept asking for you. They had almost chosen you as Mr. Fresher and you didn't feel like troubling your legs. WOW! That's great." She flared up.

"Radhika, sorry dear," He apologized again.

"I was waiting for you eagerly, you idiot! And you are so sick of us that you had your phone switched off so that no one could contact you." she burst out again.

"I had nothing new to wear." He instantly gave another reason, seeing her totally upset.

"Are you crazy, man? You sound like a teenage girl full of tantrums." She lashed out at him as she already got going.

He didn't try to defend himself this time.

"Just because of apparels, you skipped an entire memory. You are really unbelievable." She said in total despair.

"Well, if my absence created so much buzz then it's completely worthy to skip such events *na*?" He tried to lighten her mood in his typical style.

"Just go to hell, you and your weird logic," Radhika didn't seem impressed with him at all.

She hung up the phone as she really got infuriated. Earlier, she was in two minds about Kabeer's absence but when she found out that there was no such obvious reason behind it, she felt very bad and got flared up. And again with his unconventional way of handling her over the phone, she couldn't keep herself calm. As one thing led to another, she gave up on arguing further and eventually disconnected the call. He thereafter also didn't try to win her over. Even he didn't call back on that number.

*

Prevention is better than cure but cure at the earliest can also help to heal the damage soon and hence I was fully focused on the studies during that semester. Studying for me basically was mugging up. Understanding the concepts was not my method of studying and therefore I had started copying Kabeer's notes which I ultimately found to be the sure shot way for me to pass the semester.

Kabeer had his own unique way of studying. Actually, he was blessed with a million dollar memory. I am not trying to exaggerate but I seriously used to feel that he should join CBI or something similar on graduating. He was a total shocker. I had never seen him studying at length or mugging up in the classes. He just used to concentrate on the topics during the lectures and after understanding the concepts, he used to make notes of the same with the help of a reference book. He was quite disciplined in that way and perhaps that was his mantra of excelling in the examinations. Copying his notes made it easy for me to focus on the relevant and important topics mainly.

I was completing my assignment, as usual copying from that of Kabeer's, the other day. Assignments and Sessional examinations carried 25% of the total marks. And it was Kabeer's suggestion to me that completing such assignments in time would help me in scoring the passing marks very easily. I was very desperate about clearing that semester in the first go itself. So with Kabeer's assistance, I made it my habit of completing the assignments and practical work in time as I really wanted to assure myself that I was going to clear all the exams of that semester. Also, I turned into his constant bench-mate in the classroom. And he had no issue regarding that. He was happy to help me. In fact, he had always been helpful to everyone. He even used to help Lucky with his studies, who perceived him as his tough competitor. But for Kabeer, everyone was his friend.

I was busy in copying the microprocessor assignment when Radhika came to our seat. Kabeer was playing TETRIS on my cell phone. He was a gaming freak, no matter if it was off or on the field and he never used to miss an opportunity to borrow my cell phone to play the games available in it.

"Vishesh, can you please excuse us for a while?" Radhika requested to me.

"Why?" I asked.

Kabeer and I both tried to look up while continuing the activities we were doing already.

"Please!" she said innocently.

Before I could have said anything, Kabeer stood up while continuing to stare at the phone and said, "Hang on, I am coming out."

"Vishesh, make sure you complete it before I return. Otherwise, I'll not wait for you, unlike yesterday." He gave me an ultimatum by hitting the phone at my back and then took it along with him.

They went out of the classroom and started promenading in the corridor while talking.

"I am sorry," Radhika apologized for that day.

"It's okay," Kabeer replied in his usual manner.

"Nope, first I argued with you angrily and then hung the phone up without informing you." she explained the reason for being sorry.

"No issue", He said without being offended.

"No, I mean coming to any event or anywhere is totally your decision. And moreover we didn't cut any deal either and then I over-reacted over the phone that day and got carried away. So please forgive me." She further explained.

"It's absolutely fine dear, I haven't thought so deeply about it." He said as he was totally cool.

"I may be troubling you a lot Kabeer, but seriously I didn't intend to." She justified herself and continued, "I'll not offend you anymore is all I want to say. I know, we both have our personal lives and interfering just like what I did is not acceptable at all. You might have been in a relationship and all and my interference could lead to a possible issue. So from now onwards, I swear I am not going to trouble you anymore." She wrapped up everything humbly and came back to the classroom afterward.

A few minutes later, Kabeer too returned to our seats and silently sat beside me. I too had completed my assignment by then. He looked a bit exhausted. I asked him to go. He nodded his head in reply. I stood up and pulled him across.

He was in despair and silence. I asked him the reason.

While walking down the passage en route to the campus gate, he told me about their entire conversation including that phone conversation too as he would never hide things from me. He narrated the whole incident but he sounded upset. Something disturbed him, probably.

*

Radhika kept her word and afterward never tried to interact with Kabeer ever, not even by mistake. Kabeer as usual didn't bother to initiate things on his own.

I never understood it clearly how come a boy could resist his desires and feelings to talk to such a beautiful girl, who was also showing interest in him.

'Has he got some ego problem or is he gay?'

These were the only two possibilities that my mind could have thought of. But until then, he hadn't shown any such interest in me either (apart from saving my ass from Imaan sir). So it might be some ego problem with him or he wasn't mesmerized by the charming Radhika at all, unlike me. But my camaraderie with her had maintained its decorum unlike that of his. She was the same loving and caring Radhika to me. And as I already knew about their conversational agreement over 'no personal interference', so I never tried to ask her about ignoring Kabeer, neither did she choose to discuss anything about it. It seemed like she gave up on her friendship with Kabeer and it was finally over from her side. The journey which could have travelled through better paths had ended up even before walking a single step.

*

It was exam time. Practical exams were already over and everyone was busy prepping for the finals. I was even more (a precautionary measure) as I had to appear for five 2nd semester subjects along with two 1st semester backlogs but in the next coming odd semester.

I was sure about clearing the second semester but in the backlogs, I was a total zero. I thought of joining a coaching centre during the semester break to clear my backlogs but I didn't take any action and rule of physics clearly says that for every action there is an equal and opposite reaction. Well, the resulting 'reaction' was already known to me. But before any official declaration, the semester break was on and as soon as the last exam got over, I packed my bags and rushed towards my hometown in Gorakhpur.

*

After a long pause of almost 2 months, I was back to college. The feelings were mixed. I mean returning back to Delhi after spending a lot of time in my hometown with family, was really an emotional moment, but not as much as what I felt for the first time when I was joining college. And simultaneously at home, I was missing my pals along with the ambience of metropolitan Delhi too.

Life is, after all, a journey from one destination to another. The earlier you realize yourself as being a traveller, the earlier and easier you'll make peace with your life. And I was sort of hopeful about it as I returned to routine.

Well, I was none of the ones to arrive early in college, but on the first day of the academic 2nd year, I turned into one. I was delighted to meet my college friends after so long. Lucky, Sid, Anshu, Kabeer and I became best of the friends by then. We usually used to hang out together in college and therefore today I was pretty much excited as after a long pause of time, I was again going to see those heart-whelming faces together.

I met with everyone as they were arriving, but honestly, I was dying to meet Kabeer and Radhika more eagerly. Radhika arrived soon at the classroom and immediately got busy in meeting with her female friends. They seemed quite happy while hugging each other. After performing all other formalities with them, she directly headed towards me. I was eagerly waiting for that moment. She said 'Hi' to me while walking through the aisle. I replied back with a 'Hello' trying to smile as beautifully as she did. But I knew I couldn't even fake a bit of it.

"How are you? Good to see you after so long." She asked me as she reached near my seat.

"I am fine. You say?" I replied in a copybook style.

"I am also fine. And how is your family over there? Everyone hale and hearty, *no*?" she asked again.

"Yes, everyone is good there," I replied again with a smile.

Now, this was the uniqueness of Radhika. She could make everything nice and comfortable for you when she's around. I didn't remember if I had barely mentioned to her about my family, but for her that didn't matter much. She asked me as if I was known to her since forever. I felt special with that gesture of hers. She really was a beautiful person. I mean not only appearance wise but also by nature. I found myself liking her even more, just with that question of hers.

"Okay, now let me go to my seat. See you during the recess, bye." She said and turned around to go.

While turning back, she looked at the seat next to me, which was vacant. She looked at me for once before moving finally, but she didn't say anything.

Nevertheless, we were in the new classroom of our new academic year, yet Radhika (like me) too hoped that Kabeer would be likely to sit with me only. And Kabeer who hadn't arrived until then didn't turn up later that day too. In fact, he didn't appear for the whole week.

I felt like calling him up but eventually I didn't, though I was really worried about him. Actually I was absolutely an introvert person that way, who always shied away from showing his feelings and emotions. I always needed some external force to push me to get things done and that was applicable everywhere with me whether it was about studies or being social. I sometimes used to feel that I was socially challenged. I wasn't good at interactions also as I always had a sense of inferiority probably because of low confidence level and it's not only because of the reasons that I was brought up in a remote area or I didn't get to study in some Hi-fi convent school. Actually, it was more in my nature or more aptly, it was because of my inherent defects. I noticed that my father was also not a social person. Also, even my brother used to shy away from being in public functions.

You cannot change your genes or can't undo your past. But Kabeer had a saying for it. He used to motivate me by saying that, no one is perfect, everyone has certain defects and everyone is born with some possible weaknesses but promulgating those weaknesses to the world, shouldn't be your weakness. This is the least one can do to help himself, if not to overcome them.

*

Kabeer appeared in the college, a week later. He was looking all good as usual. I mean nothing harmful had happened to him physically.

He arrived 10 minutes later, after the arrival of the professor. On asking the reason for being late he told that he was at the Dean's office as he was instructed to submit his show-cause explanation regarding 1-week absence without any prior information. The professor seemed convinced with the reason and hence permitted him to join the class. The Professor, already interrupted by Kabeer, found that moment apt, to make his personal announcement.

"Class, I want complete cooperation from you as I am here only for a short span of time. I would like to enunciate that I am resigning from here very soon as I have got selected at

Delhi University. So it'll be better for us that before I resign I can cover maximum of the syllabus."

The Professor announced like a robot and then turned towards the blackboard.

"Where were you man?" I whispered slowly to Kabeer who without causing any further disturbance to the class, sat next to me.

"Homesickness," He chuckled.

'NO TALKING!!!'

The Professor warned the class without turning around and kept writing some lengthy equation on the blackboard.

"And what about you, did you enjoy your vacations or not?" Kabeer asked whispering.

"Yep, but missed college too," I answered assuring.

"Missed college or someone else?" he jeered.

The Professor turned around, shouted angrily and threw a piece of chalk at Kabeer. All done within a fraction of a second, faster than cricketer Dhoni's stumping.

"Don't you understand? I have told you not to disturb the class." He shouted again.

"Sorry sir." Kabeer stood up immediately and apologized.

"What's your name? Where have you been for the past 1 week?" the Professor questioned after getting irked with us.

"Kabeer Bhaagwat, sir. Actually, I got selected for appearing in the Army-Tech SSB examination at Bhopal, Madhya Pradesh, that's why I missed the first week of college." He again cooked up a solid story.

"That's really nice. So what's the status, right now?" Professor asked curiously as he convincingly bought what Kabeer offered him.

"Conference out, sir," Kabeer answered him in some specific terminology which I didn't get anyway.

I strongly felt that the Professor too was unable to understand the term Kabeer used to answer him and that was why he didn't try to thread any further conversation regarding it.

"That's great, young man. Keep trying further but also maintain the decorum in the class." Professor, in a relaxing tone, said.

"Sorry sir, I'll not do it again." He apologized more convincingly.

"That's the spirit," the Professor said more like a commanding officer of Defence forces and again turned to the blackboard.

While going to the electronics lab in the next period, I asked Kabeer regarding the fact of the matter.

"What's that 'conference out' and when did you go to Bhopal for that SSB exam?" I asked doubtfully.

"During the course of vacations and not in the last week," He replied focusing on my second question and left 'that' term as it was.

"Really, then why did you lie to the professor?" I asked sounding unsure.

"I wasn't even at the Dean's office either," He replied mischievously.

"What? And what if the professor will get to know about it?" I made a point.

"Professor is going to resign very soon." He winked and smiled.

*

Kabeer and Radhika were totally into that 'Promise-keeping' mode as they both had been behaving like as if no 'Radhika-Kabeer' existed in the world.

As Kabeer showed 'total no-interest' in keeping any official or unofficial relation with Radhika, people every now and then, tried to make the most of that opportunity. Well, they were not the believer of Kabeer's ideology and hence tried hard to woo Radhika. Some of them had even proposed to her for marriage. Nevertheless, there were no such things happening between Radhika and Kabeer, but a lot of speculation and conjecture was already made regarding them. And then the rifts between the two were misconstrued as some certain possibility of their love affair due to which Radhika faced a lot of criticism and troubles for no reason. People who don't get the result in their favour, at times turn into some different kind of weird species, a specimen which possesses a mind and can speak but don't use their mind to choose their words before speaking. Those rumours about Radhika and

Kabeer were generated solely by such miscreants. Kabeer who himself was a non-interfering person, was also aware of all that happening around. But as none of the chatterboxes had enough nerve to gossip about it in his presence and also as everything rumoured was baseless, he didn't bother about justifying or explaining anything to anyone. He seemed quite unaffected but problems had already started dating Radhika with fervour.

The rumours got a boost when Kabeer was seen with a 1st-year girl outside the campus, riding on his bike. Nobody said anything to Kabeer but for Radhika, things turned to worst which was bad already. And students thereafter gave her the meaningless tag of Kabeer's ex. Such continuous taunts and offending comments sooner resulted in Radhika's change of personality. As she didn't react back to people much but tolerated their bullshit for eternity fenced her extrovert nature badly. The same Radhika who had forthrightly complained against a senior, when subjected to ragging had now taken all the shit patiently over her without reacting much. The shit was after all shit and it contained nothing factual, at least I was aware of the truth but still she preferred suffering rather than bickering. Perhaps, Kabeer's silence over the matter paralyzed her. A couple of times, I personally tried to sort things out but she didn't open up to me either. I was helpless for her, like her.

*

It was our free period and I was completing my practical file copying from that of Radhika's as we were in the same group in that particular practical. It took me no time to copy it as I almost became expert in doing that. Also, she was helping me as she had nothing to do to kill her spare time. After finishing my work, I insisted her to play the game of 'TRUTH & DARE' as few of our classmates including Sid and Anshu, were already playing it. Just for fun and change of mood, I wanted to involve her in it and she eventually agreed upon it after a low resistance.

Kabeer as usual was draining my phone's battery by playing some stupid 'SAVE THE PRINCESS' mission game on it, which he had installed recently on my cell phone.

So here the game of 'TRUTH & DARE' started again after including me and Radhika as we took our seats. I spun the empty plastic bottle over the desk, around which we all were sitting forming a circle. The cap of the bottle stopped at Anamika which indicated that she had to choose between the options of Truth or Dare. Another friend Priya dared her to propose to Kabeer, as Anamika chose dare for herself. Anamika had to perform the dare and she followed the instructions given to her yet her hesitant expressions was printed on her face clearly. 'I LOVE YOU KABEER' she mumbled hurriedly as she reached Kabeer's seat. Kabeer busy in trying to save his princess was intensely lost in his game and perhaps, didn't hear it properly and afterward looked up trying to read her face in order to find out what she said. Kabeer looking at Anamika made her more nervous. She instantly looked away from him, said sorry and ultimately ran towards us. He looked at us for a while, smiled and then again got busy with his 'mission'.

Turn by turn, everyone got their respective chances as the bottle pointed out them. The last one was Radhika. It wouldn't have been the last spin if Radhika chose 'Dare' for her. But she opted for 'Truth'. Perhaps, she didn't want to perform the dare what Anamika got lately and therefore she without giving it a second thought, chose Truth.

Well, choosing truth is also a dare especially when you don't know what question you are going to answer about yourself. And moreover, she didn't want to propagate an awkward situation for herself by choosing dare as she might get a task involving Kabeer. Her intentions were honest and non-interfering but destiny had some other plans for her. The clash or confrontation she wanted to resist by not choosing dare had found its way through 'Truth'.

Sid was completely excited and therefore made everyone silent as soon as Radhika accepted to say the truth. Probably, he had some curious as well as interesting aspects to explore Radhika's life through her only and therefore he asked his question without losing a second.

"So in your relationship, who ditched the other one, Kabeer or you?" Sid asked something he shouldn't have asked.

Everyone fell silent. Not only because the question was projected at Radhika and she needed to answer it but because, no one knew exactly whether it was real or just a rumour and therefore it had always been a secret for people which they often used to talk about, privately and now they got a real chance to hear the reality from Radhika, hence they didn't want to miss that opportunity.

Well, it was a game and as per the rules of the game, the player had to perform the task honestly. Radhika had to answer for it and like a fair player, she honestly answered, "No one."

"And by the way, you have asked an invalid question?" she said in a funny way, which was actually not.

"What invalid? Don't pretend now." Sid said in an unpleasant way.

"Really Sid, there was nothing between us." She justified and further added, "We were just friends and nowadays we don't talk much, that's it."

"See Radhika, we didn't compel you to choose truth, it was your choice totally. So don't try to manipulate things now." Sid was acting stubborn for no reason.

"Sid let's leave it. Don't get carried away." I warned Sid.

Radhika looked really tensed. The feeling that she-can-cry-any-moment appeared on her face. She was kind of controlling herself from breaking down. It became an awkward situation for all of us as we didn't know how to cope with.

Out of the blue, Kabeer came out of his seat jumping over the desk, putting his virtual mission on rest and trying to save the princess in real. His face had really lit up and his eyes were doing the talking. I swear I had not seen him in that *avatar* ever before. While walking towards the 'crime scene' quickly with his long legs, he signalled me to catch the cell phone as he threw it in the air. He acted so quickly that everyone went nonplussed. Well, making a beautiful girl cry is, in fact a kind of crime.

"What do you want to know, ask me?" Kabeer said to Sid as he directly grabbed him.

Sid got a bit scared of what he had just seen of Kabeer. It was for the first time when everyone witnessing the ever smiling face was completely seething .

"Nothing bro, just for fun I was teasing her," Sid tried to defend himself.

"Really, who the fuck do you think, you are to tease her on that topic?" Kabeer said in malevolence.

I heard that 'F' word implemented from him for the very first time. The matter was really serious.

"Kabeer we all are friends, *yaar*. Chill man! We can pull each other's leg, can't we?" Sid tried to convince him for the sake of friendship.

"Really, are we friends?" He questioned Sid's statement.

"Yes bro, we are," Sid held Kabeer's hand to make an extra effort to convince him.

"Do you really think that you know Radhika so personally that you can ask any rubbish and relate it to her personal life?" Kabeer fired up.

"But buddy it wasn't even untrue, *na*? You both had a thing going earlier, we all know that." Sid argued illogically.

Kabeer now turned towards Radhika who was completely shattered by all the drama happening around. She was sitting keeping her head bent and continuously looking downwards. Kabeer moved and went up to her. He then took her hand in his and elevated her arm which was resting on the desk. With his sudden touch, Radhika shivered, what he was going to do next. I guess that was perhaps the first time he touched her.

"You all are very keen to hear that right? I am making it public now that we still have a thing going on between us and if anyone got any sort of problem with it, just tell me. I'll surely give you the best remedy for it. But from now onwards, if someone even tries to tease her or make any atrocious comment over her, I promise I'll actually make him understand how to pull one's leg perfectly." Kabeer warned everyone to not repeat the mistake.

Kabeer already holding Radhika's right hand with his left one, kept his right hand on her head very affectionately. Now that's more than enough for her to control her 'difficultly-controlled-emotions' after that heart melting gesture of Kabeer. She moved to tears without caring for the social barriers. The lonesomeness and madness she was bearing for too long had finally given up on her. Kabeer standing next to her was actually standing by her, was all I could see through my heart. She also realized the same and that was why she put her other arm around his waist and hid her face inside him. Her saviour had arrived, a bit late but it was worth the wait for her. Sometimes waiting makes the timing impeccable and relationship stronger. He proved it to her and I guess she really wanted such kind of solace only from him as she couldn't afford to pour her heart out so easily to anyone else. He was caressing her head with affection and we were wiping out tears over our cheeks.

Witnessing an innocent crying could leave you doubtful over the concept of innocence but later I realized that innocence is not a concept, it's a blessing of nature which can go in either way in several situations. But one thing is sure about it that no one can ever make you learn how to be innocent if forfeited once. Unlike most of us, Radhika still managed to retain her innocence in herself which I could clearly see through her tears. Her torrential tear flow was in no mood of taking a break and Kabeer too, didn't seem interested in disturbing her either and therefore he signalled me to bring a chair for him so that he could also sit beside her, holding her along with her emotions. I myself vacated my seat and indicated him to sit, with a hand signal.

"Radhika, it's okay dear. Stop crying now." Kabeer consoled her as he tried to sit on the chair.

Radhika loosened her clutching hand around him and then rested her head on the desk, barricaded it with both her arms. She was still not done with the emotional-water.

The lower-front portion of Kabeer's shirt was drenched as if he was sweating heavily just from there. He touched it with his palm and then showed us. His palm was completely drenched. Now it was our turn to console her or at least stop her from crying further. We tried to make her feel comfortable, but she was probably not in control of even herself. The discontent and restlessness, which had continuously grown inside her because of over thinking and solitariness, was now coming out of her heart through those tears. And it's quite natural to a human being. Being strong for too long can actually make us weak from inside. And then, a relieving hand and two favouring words are enough to break the tough shells of ours, which actually was never so.

Anyways, we all tried everything from poor jokes to imitating nonsensically to make her laugh but perhaps she was enjoying her crying act more than anything else. It seemed as she wanted to drown herself in her ocean of tears. Kabeer had still not given up on her and decided to change his approach and tried the other way around. He pulled her face up so that he could tease her. She resisted a bit but then gave up too soon. She was poorly exhausted because of that continuous crying.

"Doesn't her bloated face resemble the Genie from Aladdin?" Kabeer said funnily and laughed.

"Exactly," We replied in unison and joined the laughter.

Radhika took time to sense that she had become the centre of attention and every eye was focused only on her, but as soon as she realized it, she quickly clutched Kabeer and hugged him firmly, like a baby does to his mother. Kabeer was reaction-less as he got completely taken aback with that action. She started crying again, this time with more intensity.

"I am missing them," she said in a crumbled voice.

"Missing whom?" Kabeer asked affectionately restoring his consciousness.

"My mom-dad, stupid," She cried more mentioning her parents.

"So let's make a call to them," Kabeer suggested.

"I can't." She helplessly replied and kept crying.

Kabeer hugged her back tightly. He started caressing her head again.

He was mildly teary-eyed. *Kabeer* had moved to tears.

****

CHAPTER 8

" BOYS IN THE HOUSE"

Kabeer and Radhika made peace with their lives, to a great extent, by being friends with each other. As Kabeer didn't want to complicate things even by mistake, he confirmed and cleared his equation with Radhika and took a new initiative towards their friendship. I was really happy for them, actually, for us.

Kabeer's warning in the classroom did work in the favour of Radhika as all the rumours didn't get the required fuel to survive any more. Radhika who once was the aggrieved of such baseless rumours, afterward used to make fun of her own on that topic. Her extrovert nature bloomed again as Kabeer become a regular and integral part of her life.

Kabeer as a friend was more interesting and joyful to watch. I was sure that she actually started liking him for the personality traits he possessed, apart from his good looks. For some intellectuals, good looks are not considered as a quality but for people like me, who are mediocre-looking can explain, what they feel when they confront someone like Kabeer.

*

The 2nd-semester results were out and by God's grace, I had cleared all the subjects. Not with some outstanding marks but yet, I had managed to pass the first even-semester without any backlogs. But the ghost of the 1st-semester was still haunting me as now was the semester to cope with my earlier disappointments. I genuinely wanted to get rid of them (backlogs of maths and physics) in order to move freely in the progressing semester.

Kabeer topped the chart again with even better percentage than the previous semester, followed by Radhika, who displaced Lucky from his previous position and overtook him. Kabeer was the rising star who was shining brighter day by day and proving his consistency. He was no one-semester wonder, what some people referred to him as during the 1st-semester results. From being the talk of the town to making everyone speechless in just 1 year, he automatically got the undisputed tag of best in the business. While Kabeer was busy in winning everyone's accolades in a very shorter span of time, I still had a long way to go to be even a small piece like him. And when I say 'a piece like him', then I need not explain what impression he had left on me within a year. And therefore, I decided to push the resting position of my backlogs by his external force of teaching.

On the very next Sunday, which fell on after the day of my request to him, he invited me to his place. By then, Anshu had moved in with him to a new 2BHK rented flat, located in the vicinity next to the campus. It was my first visit and I fell in love with it at first sight, with the way the house was constructed. It was a 2-storey building with two sides facing the road and the ground floor vacant and used as a parking lot. The owner of the house was an old man, who with his wife used to stay at their ancestral home at Janakpuri. As they only visited this house just once or twice a month, they decided to give the 2nd floor on rent so that the tenant could look after their house and they kept 1st floor to themselves, for their occasional stay over there.

A rent of Rs. 3500 per month excluding the electricity bill against that awesome flat was below par its value is what I honestly felt. Kabeer had the same opinion as mine but it was their good fortune and the owner's helplessness that they were able to get such a beautiful shelter at a very low price. Well, a tenant always tries to look for a multi-facility house at a reasonable price. I again praised the architect and the artificer for constructing and furnishing it so well, as I entered the building.

A black coloured Pulsar 150CC was parked in the parking area. Kabeer and Anshu had purchased it from a bike garage owner on half the rate sharing equally the purchase-price between both of them. Though the bike was 1 user old, it was maintained so well that it had no sign of aging.

"Meet my JULIET," Kabeer observed me staring at his bike and therefore introduced me to it.

"She is a divorcee," he said very intensely, the next moment.

For a second, I wasn't able to figure out whether he was articulating about his bike or some girl who was secretly present over there. And without waiting for my reply, he again apprised me with some more facts.

"But now, I am committed to her." He chuckled.

"She's mine too, I have paid my share too," Anshu welcomed me reminding Kabeer about being the bike's co-owner.

They both hi-fived each other and cracked up.

"If I am not wrong this is the same Juliet, who was accompanying you with that 1st-year girl," I humorously added into the conversation.

"Oh! That's Aditi. She is a nice girl." Kabeer responded smilingly.

"Which girl isn't nice for a boy, Kabeer?" Anshu tried to tease him.

"Lots of girls actually," He replied back.

"People like you have always an option for themselves. But not everyone is so lucky." I tried to give them a logical point of view.

"With 'everyone', I guess you tried to refer to yourself precisely. But if you observe closely, you'll find me just like you in the end," Kabeer said disagreeing with my opinion.

"And by the way, neither Aditi nor me were trying to impress each other. It was by sheer coincidence that she met me at a local Grocery store when I was buying our daily commodities. As she was done with her household shopping as well. I offered to drop her as, I was on my bike, as a matter of courtesy. She was also loaded with big bags, so she accepted the offer, that's it." Kabeer narrated the whole incident.

"Really, but how come she got ready to take the lift at once?" I asked while climbing the last two stairs to their apartment.

"Because she already knew me, more than what I had even thought of. And courtesy goes to people like you." Kabeer said as he threw himself on the beanbag kept in their hall as soon as we stepped in.

"Because of me, what did I do?" I asked surprisingly.

 "Not you, particularly but those who love to spread rumours about girls like Radhika." He explained.

"You mean to say about Radhika and you." Anshu tried to clarify.

"You got it right, roomie." Kabeer chuckled.

"Anyways, how would you like us to welcome you?" Kabeer asked courteously once again.

"A cup of tea will do," Anshu replied to Kabeer, deciding the welcome menu for us.

"But Kabeer, I really don't think that they were purely rumours. I mean the way she treats you, is something else. No girl gives such special treatment to a just friend." I returned to the topic, following him into the kitchen.

"Why do you all try to always make a sum about it? Even Aditi sounded the same." He replied while putting the pan on the stove.

"So that we all get settled with a specific answer and it'll be easy for us to focus on the rest of the girls." Anshu replied humorously as he too entered the kitchen.

The Kitchen, in no time, turned into a meeting room. Kabeer was waiting for the tea to boil as he put all the required ingredients in it while we were waiting for his reply. He took his precious time and the next sentence that came out of his mouth was only after the tea was prepared and so was he, by then.

"In that case, you guys have all the options open. By the way, let me clear things at least to both of you. I am not after any of the girls, but if someone tries to interact with me, I can't behave as if I am allergic to them, either." He said as he poured the tea into the cups.

"GREAT!" I instantly applauded as I took the first sip. "The tea is just too good." I gave the reason of applause right back.

"This bastard is a complete package, believe me. God already blessed him with such good looks to kill the opposite sex but he still isn't satisfied completely. He wants to even bang up those souls after killing." Anshu heaped praises on Kabeer.

"Everything which is commendable is not always recommendable my friends," Kabeer said in his typical philosophical way and like always I was unable to get his philosophically heavy words. I just reacted with a meaningless smile and got busy in finishing my cup of tea.

We didn't continue with that debate over girls and good looks. I spent the whole evening over there without doing anything productive apart from helping the hosts in preparing lunch. Kabeer wanted to clear my doubts in physics but I had no such qualms as I hadn't studied any single topic and I ended up denying myself any studies. Well, it is always some other level of enjoyment gossiping with your friends about anything (except study in my case) and I was totally going with that flow.

Kabeer presented me with his physics and maths notes at the time I was leaving just like Indian folks give some gift mainly in the form of money to the guests while visiting them for the first time. And going with the same tradition, he advised me to study them instead of saying 'take care and keep coming'.

*

Anshu got a brand new HP laptop as a birthday gift from his father, and hence decided to sell his old P4 desktop system. But Kabeer came up with a fine idea of converting its monitor into a television by connecting a T.V tuner to it. We all appreciated his thought and hence purchased a new T.V tuner by equally sharing the total expense among Lucky, Sid and me. Kabeer and Anshu had already agreed upon paying the monthly rental charges of cable connection. It was purely Kabeer's idea and he managed it quite well. After all, it was a quite convenient deal for all of us as we all need some sort of entertainment and fun after those hectic classes which were keeping us more occupied as the course was progressing gradually. And that Idiot box was one of the best things for idiots like us to be entertained. And the best part was we all found a way to spend some more time together, other than in college. We usually would watch movie channels depending on the mood of majority of the present members. Comedy was the only genre which we used to watch with all seriousness so that we didn't miss any chance to laugh at the punches and one-liners. Movies, other than comedy were perpetually considered as our opportunities to fill them with intended puns, filthy dialogues and total sarcasm. And each individual always used to try to throw better punches than his contemporaries. Happiness was all we created and felt by our nonsense.

But all these nonsensical activities and kerfuffle in the house would disappear when the Indian cricket team was playing on the field, especially during the clash with the rival teams like Pakistan and Australia. Anshu and I, were not such die-hard fans of cricket in this cricket crazy nation but we were left with no other choice during such challenging matches as Kabeer, Lucky and Sid were utterly cricket crazy and they forced us to sit and watch the match along with their mood swings during the course of the play.

*

My studies and my life were going as smooth as a knife across warm butter. I had started showing improvement not only academically but personally too. I could say I was becoming a better person in the company and under the guidance of Kabeer. And it wasn't limited to only me, in fact, all of us were catching on the Kabeer effect. His conviction of keeping everything simple and straight was truly working for us, as we started believing and working on it. Life looked like an easy nut to crack at that particular portion of the time. Merry-making life, good academics, and extraordinary friends, were providing me more than what I ever thought of.

For me, Kabeer's advice and Kabeer's approval had become as necessary as worshipping Lord Ganesha before doing anything propitious in Hinduism. I found them literally as the mantra which, most of the times used to work and if not, was failsafe at least. Kabeer, my self-assumed mentor had also turned into my fashion guru. I had always been a huge fan of his dressing sense. The way he used to carry himself, had always dazzled me. His selection of apparels for his extremely chiselled and naturally toned built, always made him look very comfortable and dapper altogether. Though he could pull off any style with ease yet he was very choosy about his dressing selection. His aim for perfection could be seen anywhere, for anything, provided that he be interested in it. Sometimes I used to feel jealous of his sassiness and wanted to steal from his wardrobe but because of the difference in our dressing sizes it wasn't worthwhile either. But yes, I made it a habit to take him for my shopping trips and used to purchase based on his choices only. We would roam around a lot at Connaught Place, Sarojini Nagar and Karol Bagh for shopping or one may want to call it, window shopping. At the flea market over here, one could easily find a pretty face above the purposefully curvaceous body bargaining with a street-seller for a mere 50 odd bucks. Checking out girls there, used to work as the best recompense for us, if unable to buy anything volitional. Delhi girls always give the Delhi metro, a run for its money when it comes to being crowned most acclaimed and distinguished feature of Delhi. Meanwhile, I realized that Delhi had accepted me with open arms as I started relating myself to it. 'Delhiite', I started relating with this term proudly as I was falling in love with Delhi more, day by day.

*

Another semester came to an end like the previous ones but this one ended on a good note for me. I worked hard at my studies and my hard work finally paid off. Though it was the time for semester break and results were miles away, I was already sure about clearing the semester with a good score.

Kabeer's notes did the trick for me as it almost tore the constant company of my backlogs and me, apart. Most questions in the exam were what I had studied from as Kabeer marked them important and therefore I was confident of clearing my backlogs finally. By then, my pattern of studying had also changed. Understanding the concepts was all I shifted my focus completely on.

The examination fever was over and vacations were on like always, until the start of the next semester. I, on Kabeer's insistence, decided to throw a party for getting rid of the ominous backlogs. The *gang* was ready as ever for the celebration, but this time a grand one. Earlier we decided to spend the whole evening at SAKET, first watching some movie and then dining out, but Kabeer changed the plan at the last minute and really saved my much-needed monies at that time, with which I shopped later on, before leaving for my hometown. The new venue to celebrate the semester-end was *'DENCITY'*. (YEAH, it was named by Kabeer as he used to call his apartment the DEN and later on, the gang added CITY to it so as to mean 'DEN in the city'). He had a habit of keeping nicknames and giving an identity to everything he used to like and that was how his bike became Juliet, Radhika became Genie, Vishesh became Vishu, and then Anshu, Sid and so on.

We wanted Radhika to be a part of that celebration but as she had her train to catch in the evening right after the exam, she went straight to the railway station where her father was already waiting for her with their luggage. Her father had reached Delhi on the same day morning to accompany her while going home for the semester-break. With obliging civility, Kabeer offered to accompany her to the railway station but she being even more courteous thanked him and suggested that he have a gala time with his friends. I bet she wouldn't have said no to him any other time, rather she would've even fantasized about walking hand in hand with him for a long walk. But she was smart enough to sense and always go ahead with the clan's priorities without letting the smile fade off her face. They say 'THE FIRST IMPRESSION IS THE LAST IMPRESSION' but it is not rocket science to understand that everyone would try to be nice in the first few meets. It is these trivial things, at an uncertain and unexpected period of time, which tell about one's personality traits and moreover, the standard is nothing but the measure of one's character. Undoubtedly, Radhika was the epitome of being an ideal person.

So, we reached around 8'o clock at DENCITY along with all the 'celebrations material'. The GANG made me spend almost Rs. 1000 over it and I then understood why are students scared of backlogs. They have the potential of screwing one's valuable time along with money apart from their career. But as compared to some of the legendary identities of the college, who were still not able to clear their backlogs even after turning into an ex student from current student, I was lucky enough. Yes, it did take 3 semesters and some money in the name of celebration but now my academic past was history to me. By and large, I was happy and it made me much happier when my friends planned to celebrate this festive occasion grandly. So what if it emptied my wallet but it filled my life with some priceless reminiscences.

Within no time, we all freshened up and made ourselves comfortable in oversized tees and pyjamas which were actually a total misfit on us. DENCITY's two blokes were too tall as compared to the rest three members of the GANG, especially Anshu who was tall as well as 'voluptuous'. He had a tough built and because of which, he always reminded me of the famous character SAABU of CHACHA CHAUDHARY's comics. I always wanted to tease him, but fearing his XXL size, I never tried to. Meanwhile, in the hall, we sat around the 'partying stuff', forming a circle on a big mat placed upon the floor. Kabeer had already warned us about the 'NO LITTERING' policy, but perhaps he himself was sure that we wouldn't follow his instruction after a while, so as a safety measure he chose to make us sit on the floor for the upcoming floorshow.

"CARLSBERG," I spoke after pronouncing twice in my head.

"Add 2-3 ice cubes in it and it'll become ICEBERG." Kabeer shot back in jest. His humour already kicked off, without even boozing. Well, he was blessed with this attribute.

"Now will you mix some water with this Carlsberg?" I asked innocently to the GANG.

Everyone responded in laughter.

"Dumbo, this is beer, not whiskey, rum or vodka." Anshu volunteered to answer my question laughing.

"Don't tell me that this is your first time." Sid asked me while pouring beer for everyone into the plastic disposal glasses, which were also a part of that celebration 'stuff'.

A thick layer of foam formed at the top of the glasses as the brown coloured liquid poured out.

"So what, we are not some sot. I am also new to the business." Kabeer said to keep me motivated.

"Me too," Lucky also joined-in, in support.

"Need not worry. It doesn't affect much." Anshu said sharing his piece of advice.

"GANG, it's high time we raise a toast, Cheers to Vishesh!" Sid cheered up everyone to booze.

Everyone picked a glass for themselves but before anyone would have raised the toast, I raised my hand with the index finger pointed towards the ceiling and corrected Sid's statement with mine.

"A big cheers to our friendship as well as for our first booze-ship." I tried to rhyme and therefore added 'ship' at the end of 'booze'.

"CHEERS!!!" We all said in unison as we hit our glasses against each other's.

"It's very bitter. I can't take more." I said instantly as I sipped it and made weird faces while gulping it down.

"Grow up baby! It tastes like that only. Be a man." Anshu gibed.

"Easy Vishu easy, have some snacks with it," Kabeer told me the trick and offered me the bowl of chicken.

I tried it again after eating some butter-chicken gravy. The taste was almost the same but I liked the trick.

"Why do people drink alcohol even when it doesn't taste good?" I spoke my mind openly.

"To enjoy, to celebrate, to fake, to forget, to feel free, to relax," Kabeer gave me numerous reasons.

"And what is your reason?" I asked taking a big sip this time however my taste buds were still not impressed with it.

"I love free alcohol and food. Obviously, I am enjoying the occasion with you guys *dumbo*." He replied solving my query with sarcasm.

Kabeer's phone beeped as he completed his sentence and Anshu showed his agility by picking up his phone before him which was placed right next to him and checked it.

"GOOD EVENING SIR. HOW ARE YOU?" Anshu read the text message loudly.

"Who's that?" I asked quickly.

"His *'other reason'* to booze, the ADITI madam," Anshu replied emphasizing more on 'other reason'.

"What's up, man? What's cooking between you both?" Sid also jumped into the matter.

Boys always love to talk about girls as they are always on the top of a boy's priority list. And with alcohol, conversation on them makes a deadly combination. And going with that logic, Aditi's single text message to Kabeer was more than enough to create the mayhem among the alcoholic GANG.

"Why are you guys so obsessed with girls?" Kabeer questioned indifferently.

"Because we are boys and we are born that way," Sid answered back quickly.

"NEXT ROUND PLEASE," Anshu asked for more Brewski as he finished his share of alcohol, beating all others in the competition.

Kabeer added some more gravy into the bowl along with the pieces of chickens and offered him by saying, "Let us finish ours first."

Anshu waited patiently for everyone to finish their drinks and then started pouring beer again into the glasses, fully concentrating on not forming the foam, unlike Sid.

"See this is the correct way of serving beer." He pointed out to Sid, who had earlier served beer with frothing.

"What does she want from you? Did she indicate anything?" Lucky asked this time taking interest into the universally interesting matter.

"Nothing dude, she is a kid. She may be infatuated with me." Kabeer replied as if he was some 60 years old man.

As I was a debutant in the act of drinking, I was focusing more on eating and hence drinking cautiously, to keep myself totally in control so that the alcohol in the beer wouldn't affect me as per its actual efficiency. Contrary to me, Anshu was a believer of drinking more and quickly. His eccentric behaviour showed how easily his self-control gave up on him. And his next statement was the proof of it.

"Then why don't you make her an adult?" Anshu said to

Kabeer in reply to his statement of 'kid', coming back to the discussion.

"What do you mean by that?" Kabeer retorted strictly looking at him.

Anshu's silence was proof that he still had some sense left in him.

"Anshu is right, you shouldn't let the opportunity go waste." Sid illogically backed up Anshu.

"I think, alcohol has started affecting you both and I don't want any further discussion over this. We are here to enjoy, so please don't try to make it a wrestling ring." Kabeer reminded all of us the motto of our togetherness, avoiding any possible quarrel.

He stood up and brought Anshu's laptop from his room to the hall. He switched it on and played some peppy dance track on it. The alcohol inside us started coming out in the form of 'PRABHUDEVA'. Random songs and kinky moves from everyone were the icing on the cake. Celebration becomes huge when everyone enjoys it. It took me some minutes to realize that I was also dancing on the floor which automatically reminded me of my 1st year of college. I felt extremely embarrassed within, as the visuals started sliding through my mind. But then I started dancing again just to behave abnormally like the fellas and kept thanking God for not giving voice to feelings.

Alcohol knocked out the two most experienced boozers among us, very early in the game. Sid and Anshu fell asleep on the floor after giving their best. 'The quickly you go up, the quicker you come down', actually proved appropriate to them. We, the rest 60% of the GANG, also left the battleground and went on to the roof with the leftovers.

It was really hellacious feeling being over there. Being with your cherished friends under the jet-black sky, highlighted with countless stars and the senseless alcohol-effect, you need not ask for any such special reason to feel on the top of the world. Delhi really looks beautiful at night, especially at a height. Though I heard it many times from the locals, I was really convinced now by witnessing it or perhaps it was the same alcohol-effect again which made me admire everything. With a frequency of every 3 minutes, planes were going up in the sky, above our heads. I was totally fascinated by observing them so consistently and hence responded in claps every time as they appeared in the sky like a 3 year-old toddler would.

Alcohol is both, affective and effective in a true sense. Its bitter taste makes you feel better at times. Kabeer's advocacy to the concept of the 'other side' was really noteworthy. And it was quite ironic that I started to realize it when I was almost knocked out of my senses. In typical cricketing terms, my leg movement and hand to eye coordination were sufficient to read that alcohol had deceived me completely and I was stumped. Well, Kabeer and Lucky were still at the crease and they were tackling the alcohol-effect much better. Kabeer's cell phone beeped one more time, almost after a couple of hours. Again it was a text message as he checked taking the phone out of his pocket and happened to read out the message loudly.

"Sorry to disturb you, sir. I guess you must be busy. Good night. Take care."

Sender: ADITI

Kabeer read it exactly the way message displayed on his cell phone.

"Dude, is this serious? She really wants something from you, I guess." Lucky questioned Kabeer.

"The same thing what Anshu and Sid were saying, earlier." I, out of senses, replied.

"You guys are really sick. According to you, girls belong to either a temple or otherwise a brothel." Kabeer got angry in spite of consuming beer.

"But still, no reputable girl would keep interfering after getting such a frigid response." Lucky gave his opinion and warned him.

"It's high time to apprise her with the limits," Kabeer said to himself more than us.

****

CHAPTER 9

"FOUR SEMESTERS LATER"

A total of 3 and half years had passed. A hell lot of time had passed in a trice. And if you observe sharply, you'll find that time never comes, instead, it always goes away leaving some blissful memories and few unique lessons.

A place which had haunted me in the initial stage of my college life was now the most blissful place for me. I could easily relate it to me as I was someone peerless inside the boundary of the campus, after all. And the notion of leaving that place in a few months used to make me fervent and sensitive most of the times. I could've extended my stay there, if I was attached particularly with the college only. But I was very well aware of the fact that college would always remain there, friends wouldn't. And without those pricks, my extended stay would be the same as alphabet 'P' in 'Pneumonia'.

Kabeer was the officer-in-command, responsible for all such feelings which had generated in me for that august place. The name 'KABEER BHAAGWAT' had become a brand by then. Nonetheless, he emerged as the toast of the town ever since he joined the college but by final year, he got the undisputed tag of the 'Star of the college'. He lived up to everyone's expectation of being the most promising student of college as well. And by the way, he wasn't an overnight star. In fact, overnight success just comes after the thousands of unnoticed sleepless nights. He consistently worked towards it to prove his mettle, perseverance, and smart work, time and again and then earned that title. But contrary to his prodigal mind, it seemed like academics weren't his priority when it came to sports. He used to play tooth and nail for every single game, no matter which level he was playing. Owing to such immortal dedication, he represented our college twice as a captain of the football team at the inter-collegiate championship. Though we were purely unlucky as we lost in the finals both the times, he got his credit of appreciation. At both times, he was adjudged as the 'BEST GOALKEEPER' of the tournament.

Likewise his performance in football, he was consistent at studies too. 4 out of 7 semesters, he topped the class. The rest 3 times with a marginal difference of percentage, Lucky literally got lucky and overtook him. But Kabeer was never seen with a lament face ever for such a rat race. He was either absolutely carefree or a born masquerader. And because of that constant smile on his beautiful face, he had been perceived as a hot favourite of most of the faculty members. Some minds had the opinions that professors were a tad more generous to him and that was why he got an edge over others. But then Kabeer was Kabeer, instead of feeling bad about their comments he used to tantalize them by adding some fabricated stories about his high-level links with the college management authorities.

Kabeer was a proven prodigy who had outperformed everyone in the business already. The way he started his campaign, he was still going strong with the same steadfastness for the last 7 semesters. He was truly an undisputed vanquisher who was reigning like an emperor. But his consistency had always overshadowed the progress and improvements of his contemporaries, who had upgraded and brushed up their skills to a great extent in the journey. I could say I was one of them and raising such sort of feelings within me was quite natural because the manner in which it improved me overall, gave me an illusion or temptation of being proved superior. Well, familiarity breeds contempt and again it is human tendency to be fed up of anything which constantly accompanies them, no matter how good it is. Continuous appreciation of a beautiful face or depreciation of a not-at-par comeliness remains no longer the same because after a certain timeframe we generally get too used to it and then it doesn't remain a matter of concern for us as to how we used to perceive it in the beginning.

Now, I had started feeling the same towards Kabeer. But the irony was that the improvement and betterment I had achieved was possible because of the same person whom I was seeing now as my competition. Considering him as a competitor and a goal of beating him in my self-assumed competition had itself proven that he was way better than I. Well, he was a total inspiration, at least I could say that and the way he was leading his life taking everyone along with him was itself a big deal. I was an aspirer while he was an inspiring aspirer. My improved version had learned almost everything from him. He might not know this but he himself was an institution to learn each and every aspect of life. I might sound bizarre when I refer to all that in a context of some 20-21 years old boy but being his contemporary, I had already generated a huge amount of respect for him. And it was just his intentionally good deeds that earned him the respect, which he might not be aware of and that was another feather in his cap as a person. He was literally a router of positivity who used to emit vibes full of positivity in all the directions without fail.

What I used to feel for him, I started wanting for me too, not from him particularly but from someone who had seen me growing, improving and evolving through all those years. Day by day, I was evolving as a sensible mind but with a sensitive heart.

Everything for Kabeer was self-generated in my heart. He didn't compel me to respect him. It couldn't be possible either. The problem started as I got over-impressed with the way I came along so far in that journey, which was anyways totally mine. And I really wanted someone to notice me through all that. The pain, the suffering and the restlessness, I had gone through to reform myself into the new avatar was, I believed, exceptional. And it wasn't so that I didn't get noticed at all. I too got noticed along with the admiration of my share, but not as much as Kabeer used to get even for his trivial achievements. And that was how the word 'comparison' got introduced in my life or if I confess bluntly, I myself invited and then welcomed it with open arms keeping aside the larger than life friendship of Kabeer, which he was yet unaware of.

Comparison is the basic parameter of proving anyone superior or inferior. More-less, big-small, tall-short, fat-slim, these all are the general standards of comparison. And comparison to a limited extent, in a healthy way is inevitable. But induction of comparison in any relationship has always degraded its value. So a comparison was the new spark for me to make me shine, irrespective of the fact that it could also burn many other things if it flared up.

People usually have an opinion about others. They also have a misconception that their opinion is always right. I also had such a misconception about Kabeer in my mind. Actually, I made it more for me rather than the other way around. I started believing that I, after starting from nowhere, had come along so impeccably that I had transformed me into an ameliorated and sophisticated personality. According to my calculations, Kabeer had done nothing new to himself as he was still the same what he used to be in the initial days of college. Though he was left with nothing new to prove his calibre in but, to my one dimensional mind, it was pointless. As I had recently boarded that new flight of supremacy, it instantly assisted my already hypnotized mind in figuring out the real reason behind Kabeer being the apple of everyone's eye. The answer which was able to win over my mind after making a lot of fuss had declared him as over-hyped because he was multifaceted.

The seed of comparison which was sown in my impotent mind (by me own self) had somehow started propagating its buds of superiority, envy, mortification and much more. These ill feelings anyway require barren land to reproduce better and faster. The first time I displayed the glimpse of it was in the H.O.D, professor Bhatiya's motivational class, who had also taught us INDUSTRIAL MANAGEMENT in the 7th semester.

The Dean on the personal suggestion of Bhatiya sir, allowed him to take our motivational and personality development classes, as placements would start anytime in the middle of the final semester. Much like his personality, Professor Bhatiya's idea of teaching was totally unconventional and truly out of the box. He was more a mentor than a professor and that was why he himself took the initiative for the betterment of final year students, as we had upcoming interviews to confront during placement time.

Professor Bhatiya for the first time addressed us during his officially maiden motivational class.

"Dear students, first of all, I want to felicitate you all as you are on the verge of completing your respective courses. I know very well that one needs to give his all, over here to get a clean sheet till the end and I believe that you must have studied harder to gain that much-awaited degree, which is still a few

months away from all of you, if not carrying any backlogs." He chuckled.

"Well, any transitional phase at any frame of time is always the most vital and critical phase of life as it is supposed to be so and in fact, it really is, no matter at what age of life you are confronting it. And precisely discussing over your recent upcoming transition phase, some of you'll surely go for higher studies but most of you'll try to grab a decent job. Going for Master's Degree, more or less won't affect your current pattern of life for a minimum of 2 years but those who opt out to get a decent job after the Bachelor's degree will surely need to give their best to crack the interviews which will be held during placements.

Apart from deep and thorough knowledge of your course, good communication skills, purposeful confidence, and quick situation-reaction ability are the key elements to crack an interview convincingly. Moreover, being well-groomed is also advisable as it really adds icing on the cake. Well, attraction pulls attractiveness. And it's not bad to go for an attractive salary package if you have already decided to work for others. Because believe me friends, the world which is waiting for you, as you take the very first left turn outside the campus gate, is not so easy to survive in."

Probably the professor had a long speech to deliver but before that, I raised my hand which was a signal of interruption. Thankfully, he allowed me to interrupt him as soon as he saw my hand up in the air.

"Sir, what if we take a right turn?" I asked quickly as I stood up.

"There is nothing 'RIGHT' that exists in that world." Professor solved my query without bringing any foreign expression on his face. Apparently, it was a well-prepared speech by him and he was ready for such counter questions.

I thought I made a point but professor's epic reply proved me sheerly pointless. The chuckling response of the class did the rest of the job to bring me back to the sitting position, without adding any further ifs and buts.

"Sir, sorry to say but I personally feel that your speech was de-motivating more than what it was actually supposed to be," Kabeer spoke his opinion without waiting a further moment.

Contrary to the class's response, Kabeer stood up and took a stand but his plea sounded more like an action taken to defend his friend.

"I apprised you just with the reality, champ." Professor, without getting offended, replied.

"So by going along with the reality, I think opting for teaching as a career profession could serve the purpose quite well. I mean this is the only possible way to stay this side of the fence forever." Kabeer argued in a funny way.

"HAHA, at least you should opt for it, dear child," Professor replied as he finished his laughter.

Professor Bhatiya was a maestro in a true sense, a light-hearted fellow who loved to be in the company of students. His concept of teaching was simply to induce understanding in the minds of learners.

"Okay guys, I think this batch doesn't need any such preaching from me which is truly an achievement for me. I think we should go for a debate on any topic of your choice. What say?" Professor Bhatiya directly moved to the next episode of his class.

"WOMEN EMPOWERMENT," someone instantly suggested the topic in reply to his question.

"INDIAN ECONOMY AND UNEMPLOYMENT," another voice came.

"RAGGING IN COLLEGES," Radhika supplied this time.

"Umm... now, this is something meaty and relevant. This batch is really a gem." Professor appreciated, in fact, exaggerated for the entire batch.

"So here are the instructions. You need not split into two teams, just give your views and those who don't find them apt, can raise their hand for counter-arguments." Professor added and continued the Do's and Don'ts instructions.

"I personally believe that as a victim, there would be no one who finds ragging entertaining and supports it in any form anywhere. So our topic of discussion would precisely be 'what should be done to eradicate the beast of ragging completely?' And class, I am not expecting any pointless or illogical statements." the Professor wrapped up.

"So Radhika, why don't you commence as you have given this profoundly relevant topic to discuss upon." Professor directly came to the point and asked Radhika to initiate.

She obeyed his instructions like an obedient student and stood up. She cleared her throat as if she was going to sing some welcome song and shared her opinion.

"My dear friends, we all at some point in time, during the course of our youngest year of the college, became the victims of ragging like every batch. Well, ragging is a crime and legally a taboo but so is theft. And the irony is that they still get committed. Earlier I used to believe that punishment solely, is the best and only solution to curb it possibly. But staying almost for 4 years in the college with different sets of minds (while looking at Kabeer) I started to realize that the problem lies in the mindset. And punishment is, by the way, an after effect which actually is not a solution. I personally feel we need prevention rather than cure in this particular issue. I am not saying that I have some better and effective solution regarding this but I know, until we don't change our depraved mentalities, we wouldn't be able to curb it for sure. THANKS."

A lot of students including Kabeer appreciated her extempore speech though it landed nowhere in respect of remedy to the problem, yet it was commendable.

A sudden surge of jealousy rose in me the way Radhika looked at Kabeer while delivering her words as if he was her eye-opener. I stood up quickly without doing the formality of raising the hand and all. I am still not able to figure it out how and why, but I did something unusual and unconventional which I had never done before. I was about to go against Radhika and I finally did.

"Sorry Radhika, but I am not fully convinced by what you just said. You haven't given any proper remedy to the problem. I mean in the name of mentality mending, moral philosophy, and ethics, we just cannot be lenient and tolerate such miscreants for eternity. Etiquettes are something which should be learned during the growing-up days or schooling. After all, these are technical institutions and not some rehabilitation centres, where moral policing or counselling should be done or taught as a subject. I strictly support the policy of anyone found breaching code of conduct should be punished and rusticated. THANKS."

(ROUND OF APPLAUSE)

The intensity of the sound of the claps assured me that I sounded more convinced and forthright in my views.

"Great counter-attack, champ." Professor gave me my share of admiration too.

I was feeling gratifying and eminent of myself by speaking up my mind. Yes, it was my mind who spoke up against Kabeer's-ideology-led Radhika.

And one of the biggest thing happened was, I at least, spoke in front of so many students. Whatsoever the reason may be, but it broke the barrier of my hesitation and I convincingly conveyed what I wanted to. The impact of being in good company resulted in a good way but at a wrong timing, as I defied someone whom I always wanted to keep by my side. But I really, was on a high as I lately got to impress myself and therefore the surge of jealousy transformed into a surge of excitement. It was me who had the last laugh as nobody seemed interested in counter-attacking me. Perhaps Professor Bhatiya wasn't expecting this debate to last only for 5 minutes and hence he asked the class to confirm the same.

"Anyone wants to say something or should we move ahead? Kabeer, why don't you express your views? Please stand up."

Kabeer stood up half-heartedly on the professor's insistence, looked at me and then commenced like a professional lawyer. It looked like he wasn't happy at all, seeing me going against my best female friend Radhika's logical view. But more than that, he wasn't happy to do the same stuff that professor assigned to him. He would've left that opportunity of showing me my mistake publicly but by then, it had become a matter of right and wrong.

"Very forthright and 'remedy-oriented' speech Vishesh, I must say but it was one toned actually. Because if 'Punishment' is considered as the final and fatal solution for misconduct then I think, we wouldn't have confronted ragging anytime. Here's a thought, things are always going to hurt us, sometimes inches deeper but it absolutely depends on us what we want to take from it- a rebellion or COMPASSION.

And I quite agree with my dearest friend Vishesh's statement that professional and technical institutions like ours, are not in charge for moral policing of the students but then it's all up to individual's conscience. If we keep setting the same wrong example to our successors then should we really need to expect that one fine day, things are going to change automatically. And moreover, the motive of punishment is to make one pay for his committed sin but it doesn't assure a change in his denatured mentality.

Well, I am not in support of ragging or anything illegal. Neither am I trying to promote cowardice. But as a remedy, I personally feel that there should be some legal induction classes where seniors could freely address the junior batches or interact one to one just like this motivational or personality development class. The idea is nobody would repeatedly like to see a non-dancer dancing until it is really funny (looking at me). Same is the thing with seniors. They don't take any such interest at harassing the newcomers but they really love the fact the way juniors get scared of them. The game is all about jumping over the hurdles of hesitation, discomfort, and lack of confidence. But still the society contains some stubborn and retarded mentalities and for them, strict punishment laws should be made.

And in the end borrowing Radhika's statement, I would also say that prevention is much needed in this serious issue rather than cure because punishment is a double-edged sword which is also capable of destroying any innocent's career whereas, an improved mentality is not only an asset for individual grooming but also for the nation, in the long run. THANKS."

Kabeer signed off on a patriotic thought.

There was pin-drop silence in the classroom as Kabeer was expatiating confidently and it remained in the same state for the next few seconds even after he was done with his speech as if everyone was in a state of hypnosis or they wanted him to continue his speech for eternity. A clapping sound, finally, broke everyone's hypnotism. It was Radhika who made everyone's senses re-active just after restoring hers first. She, standing at her place itself, shouted happily while her hands kept continuing the action of clapping without fail, "Great speech, Kabeera!"

Kabeer gave her a weird look, probably he wasn't mesmerized by that modified drawl of his name.

Like Radhika, everyone including me too, stood up and appreciated him in the form of claps.

"You should definitely think of taking up teaching as a profession." The Professor complimented Kabeer jeeringly.

He responded just with an adorable smile.

And that was the epic reply from him not to the professor but to me and Radhika who once perceived him as a coward. Earlier in the heat of the moment, Radhika had mistaken him for a coward but the recent bare heart admiration for him was one of the evidences that she was wrong and now became the follower of his ideology.

On the contrary, despite knowing him too well, I was deliberately trying to commit a blunder in friendship because 'being wrong' and 'being intentionally mistaken' are two completely different things.

Though, it was a DEBATE for everyone but an absolute DEBACLE for me, a debacle for my mistaken and hitherto unproven superiority.

*

Anyways, the situation was still in control until then. The brotherhood between Kabeer and I was still unaware of any such conspiracy against it. That debate incident added another feather in the Kabeer's cap of fan following. The newest one was Professor Bhatiya, the H.O.D of the Electronics and Communication Engineering himself, who was extremely dazzled with Kabeer's sophisticated and escalating thinking and as he got to know more about him personally, he developed a good amount of fondness for him.

Professor Bhatiya and the assistant who shadowed him, used to reside in the apartment inside the campus, provided by the college management authority to faculties. His wife and only daughter used to live with the clan at their native village in Punjab because of which he was living here alone. And owing to that, we frequently used to visit him at his apartment as we got more familiar with him. His apartment used to be as organized as his life. One could barely find any possible mess there, even his kitchen used to remain clean and tidy all the time. Despite being alone, he was disciplined. Books are said to be one's best friend and he was one of those finding company among ample books. He used to read a lot of books and that was why he had thorough technical knowledge of almost everything from ancients to the aliens. His study literally looked like a study and he himself was an institution. I would've undoubtedly opted him for 'phone-a-friend' helpline if I had ever got selected for 'who wants to be a millionaire?' Gathering knowledge was his passion and sharing it was his love affair. He was really a riveting character. His oration and knowledge about trivial things were truly mesmerizing. As Kabeer started loving his company more, both, our frequency and length of stay at the faculty block, increased. Also, his affection and affability towards us used to make us feel as if we were his own children.

I was playing chess with him, one day. He was so much in love with that game that he also made me learn how to play it. Though I was a novice against him, he still used to play it with the same zeal. And as I was getting better with time, my interest in it had started growing more.

Kabeer was preparing tea in the kitchen as it had become his USP which every person close to him, knew very well about.

"So how's your project work going, Vishu?" Bhatiya sir asked while moving his 'PAWN' two steps ahead.

"Don't know sir, I don't even know what it is all about." I replied with laughter and started thinking of my next move.

"Are you crazy? How'll you complete it then?" he asked, concerned.

"No fear when Radhika is there." I replied praising Radhika and moved my 'BISHOP' on the left, diagonally to the 4th left square of the 3rd row.

Kabeer reached the hall with 3 cups of tea, kept in a plastic tray. He placed the tray aside the chessboard, on the table and threw himself on the couch.

"You too, aren't participating in your project work, right?" Bhatiya sir asked to confirm from Kabeer.

"Quite boring it is sir." He replied sounding too uninterested.

"And will it not be boring for Radhika, haan? You lazy bums are trying to fully capitalize on that poor girl's innocence." Bhatiya sir lashed out us.

"Sir, your poor girl isn't so innocent. She takes interest in such stuff, that's why." I said in a ribbing way.

"And a chocolate will be enough to repay her." Kabeer mischievously added.

We both looked each other and hi-fived chuckling a little.

"Is she your girlfriend, Kabeer?" the Professor asked curiously.

"No sir," I replied on the behalf of Kabeer, quickly.

The quick replication was automatic. It looked like an attempt to save Kabeer from further unnecessary questions which could get propagated if he would have answered for it himself. But actually, it wasn't so. Actually, after that debate incident, I just wanted to keep Radhika away from him in every possible way, even in rumours. I didn't know if I was falling for her or not but I knew that she had been in love with him ever since she saw him for the first time and it was known to everyone. The hidden thing was massive respect. Anyone could fall for him because of his captivating personality but very few of them could penetrate through that winsome body. And Radhika was one of those 'few'. The one who used to think him a coward had now accepted him in a great respecting way. She herself became the admirer and philosopher of his ideology and she showed the glimpse of it in that debate. I had seen a huge amount of respect in her eyes for him, who actually wasn't any saint but was obviously not short of a gentleman too. And a gentleman is always mistaken for a pretender, narcissist and to be having an unconventional attitude at least once. But he was actually less-selfish. He had no rulebook to follow, which could differentiate and categorize him either as completely black or fully white. He was somewhat grey, light-grey actually, who purely believed in making people benefit along with him. He wasn't a 'ONE MAN ARMY' but surely a 'SAVIOR' for few. His candidness was what he was loved for and above that he was RESPECTED.

"He has many other girls to hang around with." I gave justification of my 'NO'.

"Really, sounds somewhat like a stud. Is he?" Bhatiya sir jeered while taking a sip of tea.

"Not at all sir, he is just playing around. I don't have any girlfriend or something like that." Kabeer finally jumped into the matter and justified himself.

"No sir, there's a girl in the 3rd year, same course. She was really interested in him." I verbosely told.

"Now don't exaggerate Vishu." Kabeer gave a disgusted look and said.

"That's Aditi Sharma, sir. She is a very benignant and outspoken girl. We just went on a date once, that's it." He himself explained a bit.

"Oh! So you also went on a date with her." I asked surprisingly as I really wasn't aware of it at all.

"So didn't you like her, champ?" Professor asked taking interest into the matter.

His 'champ' reminded me of Imaan sir who must have learnt that catchphrase from our Mr. Professor only. My mind supplied the logic and justified it with professor's influential personality. I kept my 'findings' to myself and waited for Kabeer's reply.

"No sir, maybe she didn't find me at par with her expectations." Kabeer said pulling his own leg.

Kabeer never used to take it to his heart when it's all about playing around but he was very concerned about the boundary in such things. There is a very fine line between being frank and ill behaviour and he was aware of it very well. Happiness was his finest attribute. He himself was sarcastic and a fair player of it. He was same as the sender and the receiver. He was capable of beating one with his humour and made him snicker at the same moment. 'One's attire and satire should be simple yet impacting' was his motto.

****

CHAPTER 10

"GENIE AND THE GENIUS"

"Project completed," Radhika said happily to me while compiling the pages of project report in sequence.

"BRAVO!" I complimented her for taking the unnecessary baggage off our heads.

"Now it's your responsibility to get them hard-bound. The content of the first page should be well printed on the cover as our names are mentioned on it." She instructed me like a Boss while handing over some 70-80 pages of project report.

I thumbed through that unbound book and acted as if I observed it carefully.

"Where is Kabeer?" she asked me further.

"Where else must be on the ground. He is acting so carelessly as if he has no role to play in this. After all, it's his project too." I replied.

"Take a chill pill, Vishu! We are good friends, right?

And by the way, it doesn't make any 'system-changing' difference. Let him do what he loves the most." She defended Kabeer in the name of friendship.

Her reply was enough to silence me. I didn't say anything to thread it further.

"So where's my chocolate?" she said to lighten my mood.

Her love affair with chocolates was of some other level, sort of made for each other.

"I don't have one right now, but I'll gift you 2 for sure, the other one as a birthday present." I deliberately involved her birthday in my statement, which was just 2 days away.

"Awwww....So sweet of you, you remember it!" She replied affectionately extending the length of her aww. She really was happy to hear that.

"We really are good friends." I borrowed her statement intentionally to vouch for her that I was only concerned for Kabeer and not talking out of turn for him.

"And good friends are supposed to celebrate the occasion together. Isn't it?" she chuckled.

"Anything for you Ma'am," I replied and joined her in the laughter.

*

I talked to Kabeer the same day about her birthday. He remembered it too. We stressed our brain muscles a lot but reached no conclusion over the decision of how-to-surprise-her-on-her-birthday. We thought to please her with some precious gift but what to gift was again an issue in itself. Cards, perfume, soft toys... and so forth, we rejected them all. Chocolates could do the trick but surely it wouldn't remain a surprise then.

That was her first birthday with us (in Delhi) as she always used to go home (Punjab) on her every birthday. But because of project work and uncertain placement dates, she chose not to go this time, fortunately. And we wanted to seize the opportunity by hook or by crook but how? That was actually the million dollar question. Kabeer was the genius mind and hence he wanted to make everything perfect. He kept rejecting his own ideas after finding any trivial but possible deficiency. During the recess time, we were back to our pavilion aka, DENCITY as we had no classes to attend in the second half.

"Kabeer, why don't we celebrate it here at DENCITY?" I gave my suggestion hesitatingly, which just struck my mind as we reached the entrance.

"Are you sure, she'll come here? I mean will she not feel uncomfortable?" Kabeer replied unsurely.

"It's her birthday man. She can manage, I guess. It's a big day and a big reason for her to convince herself even if she doesn't prefer going to a boys' nest." I gave a reason to think.

"But still, I don't want to take even point one percent risk of a surprise turning into shock," Kabeer said involving ifs and buts.

"Surprise is meant to be uncertain and unusual. And after all our intentions are good, so it doesn't matter much. We are good friends by the way." I inserted the concept of 'Good friends' deliberately.

"What's up my boy? Sounding very logical nowadays, that day in Bhatiya sir's class also, you rocked it totally." Kabeer complimented me, which meant he was convinced and hence, was in.

*

23rd March, the martyrdom day of legendary revolutionist Bhagat Singh and also, the birthday of our own Rani Lakshmibai aka Radhika Thapar.

Our plan did work quite well as we somehow managed to evade the meeting with her till late evening. And even at dusk, only I turned up. As per the plan, Kabeer kept his phone switched off.

Everything was at sixes and sevens and our Lakshmibai as obvious, puffed up her face in anger and proclaimed it as the 'Worst birthday ever'. Even my chocolates weren't able to win her over her and as per plan I finally decided to go to DENCITY, taking her along with me. She acted as if she was totally uninterested and therefore refused, but I had to do something convincing to take her to DENCITY and hence I provoked her badly against Kabeer (including my personal envy for him). She was sulking very badly and my extra addition of fuel to the fire did the trick. We progressed across the destination to DENCITY, in the next few seconds. I kept myself completely silent all the way, in order to avoid any mishap as she was trotting mindlessly. I was following her almost jogging. I was feeling like Kabeer's opinion of turning, surprise into shock was actually going to turn true and therefore as a safety measure, I texted Anshu about our soon arrival. It was unforeseen for me and probably unforgiven for her. She as fast as lightning, was on the verge of completing her race but in the last few moments I took the lead or you can say she let me go ahead of her to guide to knock the correct door. She entered the premises of DENCITY for the first time, as I pulled one of the flaps of the main gate (which was deliberately kept open) and indicated to her, the way to go up with my eyes only. She, without waiting for me climbed the stairs quickly and asked Anshu about Kabeer, whom she met midway. Anshu stopped me at the stairs only as she expeditiously entered the hall. I obeyed Anshu and gave up on chasing. Within the next minute, Anshu pushed me across the hall. While walking towards it, I tested my 6/6 eyesight to see inside the hall but the very next moment made me realize that even human's perfect eyesight couldn't penetrate through the dark.

It was twilight by the time we reached DENCITY. The light bulbs of the house were still on rest position as there wasn't any sign of their existence. I heard Radhika shouting Kabeer's name somewhere inside the hall. They say 'anger seizes senses' or 'anger on, senses gone', and therefore Radhika in a hurry and anger mode, entered the dark and then with the help of her cell phone's torchlight, was trying to find the way inside. She was struggling in the dark and before she would've thought of coming out of the dark, Anshu yanked the door of the hall, closed and bolted it from outside. I was watching it all, clueless. All that happened in a fraction of a second. She reached to the door following the sound as it banged while closing and started knocking it insanely from inside as she might have been scared as one suspicious thing led to another. Anshu again without losing a second, rushed towards the corridor. I too followed him. He quickly opened a wooden flap mounted on the wall of the corridor and restored the electricity, which was already tripped through Miniature-Circuit-Breaker, commonly known as the MCB. We again ran towards the already closed entrance of the hall. The shouting and the knocking at the door had stopped by then. I was in the state of bewilderment but somehow my hands seemed unaffected amidst that sudden shock process and they themselves opened the door as if they operated on their separate nervous system other than the natural & common one. Lights were on now and so was the fan. The floor was completely covered with the petals of several coloured flowers, which were making some random design as they fell off from the ceiling fan which started rotating. I looked at the ceiling. Along with the fan, more than a dozen of red and white heart-shaped balloons were suspended below it. Kabeer was standing against the hall entrance, wearing a conical paper birthday cap. Behind him, 'HAPPY BIRTHDAY GENIE' was designed by cutting and then pastimg some coloured papers over the wall. Below that GENIE, a '☺' smiley was also designed.

Radhika was sitting on the floor, next to the door bowing her head downwards. Her legs were folded and both the arms were resting across her knees. She had hidden her face between the arms. A few petals had landed on her head too. Silence had completely dominated over everything else present in the hall except the fan suspended below the ceiling, which alone was trying to give a run for the money to the monopoly of silence by continuously producing rumbling noise while rotating. Everyone was frozen in their place as nobody had enough nerves to ask anything to Radhika, yet. I tried to initiate as someone had to and moreover it was my idea to surprise her. I tapped her shoulder.

"Radhika are you okay?" I asked hesitatingly.

She nodded her head in reply which was YES, but not actually.

"HAPPY BIRTHDAY RADHIKA", Sid and Lucky said in unison as they appeared just in time, with a big cake packed and wrapped, inside.

'That must be a part of the plan.' I thought in my head. From what I knew, surprising Radhika was all about bringing her to DENCITY without letting her know about our secret celebrations plan. I managed to do that suitably. But after reaching over there, I was also as surprised (or shocked) as she was. 'What next', I was trying to continuously think of.

Radhika raised her head up as she heard voices of Sid and Lucky addressing her. I tried to look at her face curiously but contrary to my opinion she wasn't crying. She stood up quickly with anger filled in her eyes. Her fiery eyes reminded me of the third eye of Lord SHIVA which is supposed to be located at the center of his forehead and generally remains closed (which I had read and also seen on the T.V.). Its prime function is supposed to demolish sinners and demons. We also were about to be incinerated.

"Who was the mastermind behind all this?" She spoke for the first time in the last 10 minutes, giving an intense look to everyone.

"Sorry Radhika, It wasn't meant to disrespect you. I am really sorry." I apologized beseechingly.

"So you planned all this?" She directly came to the point looking towards me.

"Genie, we wanted to plan a surprise for you, but all this nonsense was the produce of my rotten mind. Don't spoil your mood, *na*. They all are here just for you. Please! I am extremely sorry." Kabeer, embarrassed and apologetic tried to outdo the chaos created already.

Kabeer while ending his statement had already turned towards the wall behind him. He knew he had pressed a wrong trigger as his surprise resulted in an absolute failure. He was already unsure about taking the risk and it actually cost him heftily. He realized that he had spoiled the celebrations and the mood on Radhika's big day and he showing his back to us meant a big mess. We all automatically set ourselves on mute mode.

"I knew this must be you," Radhika said while walking towards him.

"I am sorry Radhika, I am feeling really bad." He said again being apologetic and kept both hands over his forehead while he kept looking at the wall. He was surely looking either at GENIE or that smiley, he had made with paper, I reckoned.

"You almost killed me and you are feeling bad. My heart was about to come out of my mouth, you fool." She said while pulling him towards her.

"I am sorry, *na*." His voice crumbled.

"Awww.... this lad can cry too, I thought he just loves to pull a gruesome prank on others." She teased while holding both his hands.

For a moment, I didn't believe what I heard. I thought she was just messing with him but when I personally checked him out, I really found him teary-eyed. It was once in a blue moon moment, which is supposed totally against one's male ego but completely justified as a human being.

"Kabeer, I was just playing around *yaar*. Just the way you did." She said to bring back things to normal.

She almost made us feel guilty for some 15 horrible minutes and then she was justifying it by saying that she was joking. Kabeer said nothing and kept looking downwards. A tear with the intensity of destroying everything fell down. His repentance was speaking through actions now.

"Are you crazy or something, Kabeer?" she scolded him affectionately.

He had nothing to reply. He was continuously gazing at the floor or probably at her feet. She waited a while for him to reply but couldn't resist herself for long and finally, she went close to him. He didn't bother at all to look up. She, without waiting further for any of his approval, came on her tiptoes and hugged him. She was 5'6" tall, yet she needed to put an extra effort to hug him properly. He hugged her back firmly, totally surrendering himself. It looked like he needed that hug very badly in order to get convinced that she was really joking and not pretending. Perhaps the way she hugged, brought him that much-needed feeling of content. His face was towards us and the tears which were not allowed to leave the brink of the eyes had mutinied now.

"I am sorry, I spoilt your day." Kabeer sobbed.

His eyes and nose instantly turned red because of crying.

"Actually, you hugged me, you made my day." She corrected him.

"I am really sorry." He apologized again while wiping away his tears like a kid.

"Actually I need to say sorry right now as I can't stand like this for long." She replied funnily.

"Thanks and Happy Birthday Genie," he whispered before loosening the hug.

"Thank you." She planted a kiss on his cheek, out of the blue.

Kabeer's empathy for Radhika was the reason behind

the tear fall but she didn't kiss him because of sympathy. Her reason of kissing him was those priceless feelings she had been carrying with her since they'd generated within her. And seeing the tears of the engenderer of those feelings, it was very tough for her to cease herself from hugging the person probably she loved the most. Though she never said it anytime yet she expressed it many times. I was aware of it, at least. But she wasn't aware of the fact that now I wasn't comfortable with it.

Her closeness with Kabeer anyhow was enough to make me feel jealous. It had become unacceptable for me and since I had started minding it too much, it had started affecting me proportionally. The reason was also not clear to me but probably because my itch of gaining superiority had already perceived her as the only medium through which I could've proved my transcendence, by surpassing the best. I was already a known identity in the campus but that was again because of Kabeer and to come out of his shadow, I needed to achieve something big, which could make headlines in no time. And having a partner like Radhika was a big achievement in itself. Though it was Kabeer who didn't change his status of a friend with her into a relationship but still she with me could make a totally different story. Girls like Radhika, happen to meet once in a lifetime and I knew I wasn't so lucky to get even the shadow of her again if missed the opportunity right then. Though she saying yes to me, I couldn't imagine even in my wildest of dreams but fortunately, she had always been a good confidante of mine. So chances were there as it was a different kind of camaraderie between us and according to the then me, it is quite logical to fall in love with someone after being more than just acquaintances first and then getting attached to them. That is a quite practical and secure way of loving after being aware of their pros and cons very well.

Getting Radhika into my life could have served me two purposes simultaneously. It was more like killing two birds with a stone. And moreover, the way I was getting obsessed with her, I felt it was my love for her.

SURPRISE is the pleasant feeling just like 'unwrapping a gift' and SHOCK is like 'coming to know that it wasn't a gift for you'. The idea of surprising her was mine but it ended up on a shocking note for me. And the shock therapy didn't stop there at all. The night had hidden some more eggs of both, shock and surprise in her womb.

The cake cutting ceremony was over. We, the GANG had arranged a small party for her, equally contributing our shares. Radhika really seemed pleased with our efforts. She had gotten some real 'AWWW' moments too as she felt very much valued and even cried in between as the night progressed. Sid and Lucky departed after feeding themselves up to their necks. They were very well aware of the fact that they were also the shareholders of the food we had ordered and that was why they fed themselves with every possible eatable they didn't even need to, as if there was no tomorrow.

It was 30 minutes past 9 and Radhika was all set to go. Anshu out of the blue came up with an offer of boozing.

He asked Kabeer to buy beers while returning back to DENCITY after dropping Radhika to her PG. I endorsed Anshu and hence decided to stay over there at night. Kabeer easily got ready for it too and with 3 out of 3 votes in the favour, we decided to party hard.

Suddenly, Radhika too walked away from her plan of going back to her residence and she wanted to booze along with us. Now that was quite an unprecedented situation for us but one thing which I damn sure about was, if she stayed, Kabeer wouldn't allow anyone to drink. I was well aware of his very little but totally restricted DON'TS and hence my excitement vanished in a second or two as he said the same and the plan remained just a thought. It would be final if there were only boys in the house but we all forgot that that night we also had a girl among us and in such cases, Girls are supposed as the final authority to approve the plan. And one cannot obtrude anything on a girl especially when it's her birthday.

Kabeer, for fun, deliberately insisted Radhika join him to the beer shop, as she showed extreme enthusiasm to drink too. But she put down his offer with a very strange reason for not wanting to get on the bike particularly with him. Hence Kabeer and I rushed towards the alehouse hastily as the clock was about to strike 10. Delhi has a system of 'NO-LIQUOR-AFTER-TEN'. Though we used to have enough links to black marketers, yet Kabeer was completely focused on sending Radhika back to her nest and therefore he wanted everything to wrap up soon. The need and the demand of the time were to beat the clock and we eventually managed to do so as we reached there in the nick of time and got our stock, a tad lesser though than what we asked for but it was still manageable. By then, I had increased my drinking capacity too. I 'improved' that way too.

Anshu had arranged some more snacks (in addition to the leftovers of what we ordered) by then. Radhika too had prepared some salad of onion and cucumber which by-chance she found inside the refrigerator. And when I am confidently saying that she prepared the salad, it's just because the way it was decorated and served. Also, the mess we created during the cake cutting ceremony was cleaned up and the hall was organized beautifully. Girls are quite formulated that way, I must say.

*

Radhika managed to drink an entire 650ml bottle alone despite being a debutant with us. Her performance was really better than that of mine in the maiden booze party. Anshu who was quite experienced in it, as he used to claim, started losing his senses as usual and stood up. He did some dance steps (perhaps taken from his regional dance) along with some melodrama and then went straight to his room as he got a call from his girlfriend who was thousands of miles away, somewhere in Bangalore.

My capacity of boozing had grown but not the tackling skills and as I reached the half of my second bottle, I too started deviating from normalcy. I literally wanted to test my flying skills as the Brewski developed an urge of flying, inside me. I even went to the balcony to dive from, but it was stupid Kabeer who was jealous of my wings of high spirits and pulled me back to the hall. He was also one bottle down but did not seem affected that much otherwise he would also have given a try to flying.

As Kabeer brought me back to the hall, we found Radhika communicating with someone over her cell phone. He intelligently kept his hand over my mouth and made us stop at the entrance only, as a precaution. We waited like that for at least not less than 10 minutes till the conversation ended. It was her dad's call as we reckoned listening to her and she was literally enjoying telling every single thing to him with the silly details and then after talking for eternity, she hung up the phone on a good night note. Probably she might've lost her mental balance and that was why she wasn't able to sense the reality. The cruel alcohol had landed her in a big mess. And why do girls take an entire era when they start talking over the phone and that too, regularly with their folks? I mean I don't remember any single time I have called up my family and my call details have shown even some 5 minutes of conversation at a stretch. Even I never saw Kabeer communicating too much over the phone with his mother, though he was much attached to his family. No, I am not claiming girls as talkative but they are too descriptive.

"Were you talking to your dad, madam?" I asked wondering as soon as Kabeer removed his hand from my mouth.

"Y-E-P, do you have any problem with that, sir?" She retorted back following the salutation I started.

"No, not at all but do you remember, you told him about being here, with us?" I said as my alarming senses were still active.

"So what, he already knows about you guys." she replied with the utmost carefree attitude.

"How come? Have you ever told him about us?" Kabeer was dumbstruck with that revelation and hence jumped into the conversation by asking that silliest of questions.

"Yep, He has seen you. He even liked you." she winked at him and replied laughingly.

"When did he manage to see me?" He further interrogated her to find the clue.

She didn't reply for a while as she fell silent and goggled like an owl. I knew alcohol couldn't go wasted especially when it had to impact someone unseasoned. It reacted a bit late but completely slacked her nervous system. She looked like as if she was trying to recall something very hard but not was able to.

"I showed him our photographs, *na*. Well, I don't hide anything from them." She replied after thinking too much.

"Did you also apprise him with the truth that you are drunk?" I curiously asked this time.

"HEHE... you guys are so pigeon-hearted. Chill boys! I am not a kid and by the way, it's my birthday, so we are allowed to booze a tad." She replied while standing up and then started spinning at the same place.

"Genie, it's too late now. Let's go, I'll drop you home." Kabeer instructed 'Genie' to pack up.

"No never. I am not going to sit on that stupid bike with you anytime." She said in a resistant manner.

"That's Juliet, not some stupid bike. And by the way, what problem do you have with that 'black beauty'?" He took a stand for Juliet and argued.

"I know, girls are dying to ride with you on that Juliet or whatsoever but not me. Better, keep that seat reserved for your girlfriend only." Radhika started drawing fire taking the assistance of alcohol.

"I don't do any charity like that and I don't have any girlfriend either." Kabeer irked and retorted.

"But you also don't deny them, you big-hearted bloke." She was prepared for her next move.

"Who the hell are you talking about?" Kabeer all fed up of that no-reason argument, said getting more irritated.

"I don't know there may be so many." She kept stuck to that indirect mode and didn't respond properly.

"OKAY! Lemme get an auto-rickshaw for you." He gave an alternative.

"See Vishu, how easily he has accepted his depraved act of flirting?" she dragged me into the debate or rather argument. She wasn't even happy with the alternative option.

"What do you want me to say, Radhika? Please make me

understand." He said as he had totally given up on that pointless topic.

"That 3rd-year girl, she was riding with you on your bike, right?" She finally revealed the secret with a delay.

"That's Aditi and it's been ages to that incident." He confirmed her identification to Radhika (which she already knew).

"Whatever." She acted as if she wasn't interested in knowing her name.

 Why do girls react like this? I mean if some random girl happens to get linked with the person they like, then why the hell do they act like as if they don't give a damn about it, especially in front of that particular person whom they like. Though they would have already collected entire data about them, without bringing it to their notice so that on doomsday they get the opportunity to tell him why he is facing different consequences.

I don't know if a man also does such snooping because till then, I was still addressing Kabeer with his name only unlike the girls who decided to not address the elephant in the room.

"Should I go to drop her?" I offered a solution to both of them.

"Should I call an ambulance, before that?" Kabeer instantly made me shut my mouth automatically.

"Bring me that bottle of beer. I am going to the roof." Radhika who was not interested in going home said pointing towards that untouched single bottle left with us.

"I am also coming, Radhika. Bring mine too." I ordered Kabeer for my half-emptied bottle and followed her.

"Bring Anshu too." She added in the order list while climbing the stairs to the roof.

Kabeer was now totally in a mess and I was really enjoying seeing him like that. He used to address Radhika as Genie but right then he himself had turned into one and hence bore all our tantrums without arguing at all. I was well aware of the fact that when he used to take responsibility, one need not think twice before doing any stupidity of any level.

Following all the orders literally like a 'Genie' (except bringing Anshu as he must've fallen asleep), Kabeer reached up with 3 bottles of beer holding in his hands and a mat over his shoulders. While keeping the bottles down on the surface, the mat dropped off his shoulder automatically. Radhika and I were already sitting at the front-left corner of the roof and therefore Kabeer stood next to us silently after unfolding the mat. He himself chose to stand leaning against the iron railings of the roof on the front end while the other three boundaries were cemented walls. He took out a cigarette from the cigarette box (which actually belonged to Anshu) and lit it.

"Hey, do you smoke too?" she questioned him curiously while moving over the mat.

"Kabeer, do you..?" I repeated the same question with same intensity following her activities.

"It's your birthday, after all. We all are allowed to do anything we feel like, I guess." He replied with a not so surprising answer as per his style.

"Why do you always do that, TIT FOR TAT?" She questioned back.

"Why do you judge others on every single thing?" he replied with another question. At times, he was totally a different person altogether.

"I love you Kabeer. You brought another bottle for me." I said affectionately as I picked the sealed bottle of beer.

"Keep it down, that's not for you. You finish your bottle first." He reacted sternly.

"But I still love you, bro. You know, you are so empathetic and benign. You always act as a helping hand to everyone and are not like me. I am a bad apple who is totally self-centred." I said as I picked my bottle and took a huge sip of my share, which almost emptied the bottle.

Alcohol inside me had started dominating over me. Not me actually, over my ego. And because of which the innocent me was set free from the vault of pretence. The soul somewhere inside me, knew what was exactly right and what was completely wrong and eventually the alcohol all inside me had provided it a medium to speak up. Tears were my speech. Yes! Now it was my turn after Kabeer. I always knew I had deliberately taken the access to the wrong track and the ego-less me was then feeling guilty for it, which was my reason to sob.

The 'comparison factor' which had taken a permanent seat in my mind, also knew that I was not up to it as much as Kabeer and therefore I automatically started counting his spectacular attributes, which I didn't possess. My tears were the proof of my acceptance of being secondary to him.

Kabeer threw his fag-end and immediately came near to me. He started sympathizing while seeing me cry.

Radhika was on a different mission altogether and she emptied Kabeer's half-filled bottle meanwhile. It then became next to impossible for him to nurse us simultaneously. Though we kept our asses glued to the mat only yet we didn't let any opportunity go waste in messing with him badly. He sat between us so that he could hold both of us but on the contrary, we held on to him from both sides. He kept my head on his right shoulder and kept tapping my head as I was crying and to his left, Radhika had already held his hand firmly. I asked him to loosen me as I wanted to tell him something. He did so only after taking assurance from me that I would not create any further mess.

"Kabeer, you know you are very beautiful," I said while pulling his cheeks softly.

"Really!" he calmly replied.

"Yes, my bro. You really are! Not only at heart but your total aura is." I said and placed a kiss on his right cheek.

"Ahaan... How much?" he asked unnecessarily just to continue the conversation and made me lie down, putting my head on his lap.

"Very much, if you were a girl then I surely would've proposed to you," I replied as I was on the verge of entering into the virtual world.

"No issue at all, we'll let this bromance continue by being legitimately bisexual." He replied in an illogical manner for my illogical statement.

"Shut up. What problem have you got with the sex opposite to yours?" Radhika intervened our future planning by shouting and simultaneously pulled him towards her by grabbing his T-shirt from the shoulders.

My head which was resting on Kabeer's lap got displaced and eventually came onto the floor as he with a sudden jerk, went over to Radhika. Fortunately, to an extent, the mat acted as a cushion to my head and prevented any serious injury. My mind which had totally surrendered itself to sleep came back from the virtual world to real for a trivial span of time. Kabeer groped my head and asked me if I was alright. I wanted to reply but the inebriation of alcohol causing sleep didn't let me and took over me completely.

*

Next morning, I woke up around 10'o clock when Kabeer came with a cup of tea and shook me. I then realized that I was on the bed. It was Anshu's room. On asking, I got to know that it was Kabeer who brought me there in the night after I fell dead, figuratively of course, by sleep.

His eyes had turned completely red because of sleep deprivation, which embarrassed me when I recalled the previous night's nonsense act by me. He was quite okay as he had no complaints to make against me. I asked about Radhika. She had already left for her P.G. home as Anshu had dropped her early in the morning.

Kabeer wanted to sleep soundly as he hadn't slept for a single second at night. I, after having my tea, left DENCITY.

*

I ran into Radhika in college the day after the next day. She seemed quite pleased as if she was still hungover from that merry frolic birthday night. Also, she was all praise about the GANG, the way we celebrated her birthday. However, she pulled my leg a lot by imitating me and reminded me of the minute nuances I created unwillingly after boozing. She laughed all day remembering the incidences and above all she was enjoying herself by acting the way I cried that night. All in all she was happy.

Kabeer, on the other hand, was quite lost. He appeared totally droopy, not as enthusiastic as he usually used to be. We found him in an intense mode, brooding all day. It seemed as if something inside his mind was nagging at him without a break. I asked him what I sensed but he procrastinated. Believe me, he sometimes, was really impossible to understand and then you couldn't prise out of him anything if once he decided not to speak his mind. He was really a hard nut to crack in such cases. At times he used to become so manipulative that in the process of probing him, one would eventually end up undignifying himself. Well, manipulation is an art. No one can be right all the time and that is how manipulation steps in. His silence raised a few questions and also put a question mark on me. A speck in the beard of the thief was the idiom that completely suited me right then. I had my fears. Alcohol can screw you. But fortunately, I wasn't the reason behind his change of behaviour. It was probably Radhika's over-expectation troubling him again as she had never shied away from expressing her love for him openly but fear of losing him, had always forced her to take a back seat. But now when she realized that she was equally as valuable to him as he was to her, maybe she wouldn't have given a damn to confess what she exactly used to feel for him. Though I didn't remember much of her saying any such details to him that night, neither Kabeer was ready to disclose anything, but it was all I could reckon to be the possible scenario.

And if it was so, then it really would have been the worst news for my 'SECOND TO NONE' mission. My egoism and absurdity took over the 'Alcohol-less-me' again.

****

CHAPTER 11

"HISTORY REPEATS, PAST SPEAKS"

2nd APRIL 2011

INDIA v/s SRI LANKA

ODI, CRICKET WORLD CUP FINAL

India under the phenomenal captaincy of M.S. Dhoni along with some clinical performances of the squad, throughout the tournament, went on to the tournament final after outperforming all other opponents.

And today was the finale, the Grand-one, between the two Asian teams who proved themselves better than their other contemporaries. The first time when Indian cricket team lifted the World cup, was 28 years earlier. I wasn't even born then. There is a saying that History repeats itself. And believe me, the Indian cricket fans were so desperate that they were literally praying for this 'saying' to turn true. Kabeer was one of them, I could easily say without doubting his immense love for that sport which is also known as a religion in this country. Contrary to him, I was purely an atheist to that religion and he knew it very well yet he deliberately took me along with him to DENCITY after submitting the final copy of our project report in college. On that day even our college didn't look like the regular one and I could bet my bottom dollar that it would have registered the lowest attendance of students on any academic calendar day. Lucky and Sid too, didn't turn up to college because of that most trending game on the television.

Sri Lanka, after batting first, put a good total of 274 runs capitalizing on a well-struck century of their star performer Mahela Jayawardne. It was break-time for the two teams and also for the television-viewers as the channel switched their telecast from the live action on the field to the experts' opinion in the studio. Anshu who already fell ill because of the change in climatic conditions found it the most appropriate time to remind Kabeer to accompany him to the Doctor's clinic.

Summer had almost arrived in commence of April. Delhi has a variety of seasons. Delhi, actually, has a hell of a lot of varieties in everything ranging from its food to its mood. And that was one of the prime reasons why I was so much in love with the city and on an honest note I had already declared myself a Delhiite by then. It was just too cool for me to get known as one. But right then, Anshu's health or precisely his stomach's mood wasn't so cool. Due to warm weather, he suffered from diarrhoea and the it had made him weak and helpless in a few hours. Kabeer and I, both fought over the decision of who should go with him as we both didn't want to go. He had a solid reason for the on-going cricket match whose second innings was about to start while I had no such excuse to present. Though I really had no issues over leaving the company of that idiot box I was sitting against but actually I didn't want to go alone, I mean without Kabeer and therefore I then started blackmailing him by giving sentimental excuses over my forceful presence at DENCITY, just because he wanted me to be there and watch the entire match along with him. After throwing and receiving plenty of tantrums at both the sides, by and large, we agreed upon the alternative solution of accompanying Anshu together and the three of us finally visited a nearby private clinic. After a short check-up, the doctor prescribed some medicines and also advised him to take liquid diets only. While paying his consultation fees of 100 bucks, he handed us down 2 packets of oral rehydration solution for free as a great gesture of generosity. Anshu came out of the clinic with a mouthful of ill words for the doctor who made him pay 100 bucks for 10 rupees items.

While returning back to DENCITY, we purchased those prescribed medicines and a 1litre tetra pack of REAL mixed fruit juice from the local medical store. Anshu felt like consuming some juice as he was on empty stomach since morning. After drinking a small amount from the pack, he handed it over to me as we were riding on the bike. I had fit myself somehow on the bike because of Anshu and Kabeer who captured the maximum share of the seat with their respective bigger bodies. Kabeer was riding the bike whereas Anshu was in the middle and therefore I was sitting more on any imaginary seat in the air rather than the actual one, which had no room for me to sit properly. Anyways as soon as the juice pack was handed over to me, I drank from it too but a tad more amount than what Anshu drank. Besides being in that condition, he shouted at me with all the energy left in him and presented me my share of abuses. I, in order to tease him more, opened the pack and drank again.

My stay at DENCITY got extended for the time being as Kabeer requested me to do so. In reality, I wanted to leave, but his alluring proposal of boozing at night, made me change my rapacious mind and hence I stamped my confirmation for an overnight stay to the perpetual convincing puppeteer, Kabeer Bhaagwat.

The word 'Beer' in our conversation also fell in the big ears of Anshu, who directly went to the washroom as soon as we reached DENCITY. Though he was totally in bad shape yet his urge for boozing had remained unaffected. He took the word 'LIQUID DIET' too seriously.

Meanwhile, in the game, Sachin departed as we arrived. India was 31 for 2 wickets as both, Sachin and Sehwag, one of the most destructive opening pair was back to the pavilion.

"I can bet everything on India that they will end up as losing side likewise in 2003." Anshu teased Kabeer while coming out of the Washroom.

"Shut up you OMINOUS idiot. At least have a heart." Kabeer talked back citing our unnecessary visit to the doctor because of him.

"You better go to your room and rest." I gave him the best piece of advice I could.

I thought he would again open his mouth and throw some real shitty words at me, pun intended. But defying my thinking, he silently stood in front of the television for a couple of minutes and then went to his room. He was really exhausted, I guessed. No, he came to the hall just to criticize the Indian cricket team and to take his juice pack.

Virat Kohli and Gautam Gambhir were on the crease who played some sheer excellent cricketing shots to take India to 114 in the 21st over before Virat was caught and bowled by the right-handed spinner Tilakaratne Dilshan. After Kohli's wicket, Kabeer decided not to watch the match (because of some self-made superstition of his own as he desperately wanted India to win) and therefore went to the kitchen to prepare dinner but nevertheless continued asking me the score. I didn't know how and why, but for some unreal reasons, his voodoo actually worked as long as he cut himself off the television. The left-handed batsman Gambhir and skipper Dhoni added 109 runs for the fourth wicket and made the chase quite easy. Gambhir was playing on 97, just 3 runs short of his grand-century. Hitherto, Kabeer was also done with the dinner preparation and hence he came out of the kitchen with two chilled beers (the stock of which he had already purchased and kept in the refrigerator), handed both of them to me and himself stood impatiently in front of the television to see Gambhir finish his century. Keeping his hands on his hips, his eyes were totally staring at the television to watch the result of next coming ball bowled to Gambhir. And Kabeer jumped.

"Fuck man!" He shouted in anger & agony as Gambhir had to leave the crease.

"Bad luck." I also restricted myself to just two words to express my feelings.

"He was playing so fucking well, *yaar*. Couldn't he wait for 3 more fucking runs?" He shouted and opened a bottle of beer which I had placed on the table in meantime.

The word 'FUCK' used twice in two straight sentences by him was almost like a wonder. One couldn't easily hear foul words from the too civilized and well-spoken Kabeer. He turned angry as Gambhir missed out his well-constructed and well deserved century. But what was done couldn't be undone. Next was the stylish and in form all-rounder Yuvraj Singh who came to the crease as 52 runs were needed off the next 52 balls. Now was also the high time for the skipper M.S. Dhoni to do his bit as he was already looking too impressive with his bat. Going along with his reputation he soon started firing, which he used to be best known for.

In the next half an hour, we too reduced the level of our ravenousness as India reduced the chasing target and needed just 4 runs off 11 balls and our skipper was on strike. There wasn't any doubt left in anyone's mind that India had sealed that much-awaited victory and just a formality was needed to be done to officially emerge as the winner of Cricket World Cup 2011. SIX! The very next ball went to the far end of the ground and the Indian skipper finished off the match in his unique style.

And that 'SIX' by the skipper introduced celebrations in the blood of the nation. Yuvraj hugged Dhoni on the ground and Kabeer hugged me off the field. Finally, we did it. The prayers of billions of Indian cricket supporters had been answered. It was really unbelievable but it was a new history. A record was made by breaking many others and the sky immediately filled displaying fireworks more than its own stars it housed. Kabeer was on Cloud Nine as he was jumping, shouting, crying and finally when he found himself unable to control his expressions of gratitude, he started shaking his other bottle of beer as if it was champagne.

"JIYO DHONI!" Kabeer hailed the Indian skipper somewhat imitating me as I often used to appreciate him like that especially when he used to do something exceptional.

Kabeer was completely lost in the celebration process while his cell phone rang. He was deliriously happy and reached ecstasy as India won the world cup. He was behaving as if he had attained the state of NIRVANA and he had nothing to do with this materialistic world. When I informed him about his ringing phone, without coming out of his celebration mode, he casually asked me to check it out as he had messed up his hands with slopped beer. It was Radhika's call. He asked me to put the phone on speaker as I told him.

"Kabeeeeer, we won the Cup." She shouted as quickly as the line got connected.

"Yep Genie, We did It! Ummmuaahhh." He shouted using all his energy, from our end and blew a long kiss over the phone.

Did I hear it correctly? He blew a kiss to Radhika. What does that mean? Is he trying her to give some possible hints? Or are they already into something?

A flood of questions knocked at the bolted door of my mind. Before I could have counted some more ifs and buts in that complex equation of love led by friendship, Radhika made the equation simple for her and me (unknowingly) too, by asking the same doubt.

"Kabeer, what did you just do?" She asked curiously but her voice wasn't able to hide her excitement.

"Ummmuaaaaahhhh. Can't I kiss you?" He again blew a kiss in the air and threw the ball in her court.

Usually, he wasn't too expressive regarding his feelings. But that was obviously a big occasion for him to not hush up and at the same time he was too street-smart because of which what Radhika wanted to get assurance from him, but she needed to answer now.

"Kabeer, it's quite late. I think I should sleep, we'll talk tomorrow. Good night." She, in a single breath, said and hung the phone up.

"Good night, Genie." His reply came after the line was disconnected. He winked at me and then went to wash his hands.

We resumed the celebration, though I was offended. The post-match ceremony was on the TV and it was the time to announce player of the match award.

"What say, Gauti or Maahi?" Kabeer asked me as if he had spun coin in the air and I had to choose between heads and tails in context of Gautam Gambhir and M.S Dhoni.

"Gambhir should get it." He answered himself before me.

"I'll go with Dhoni. After all, he has finished the game with unbeaten 91 runs." I gave my opinion, which was honestly an attempt to differ with that of him.

We didn't have to wait much for the announcement and coincidentally, the awarding jury came up with the same opinion as that of mine and they picked Dhoni as the player of the finale.

"Gambhir performed well in extreme pressure situation. He should've got this." Kabeer said not agreeing upon the selection.

"Because he is a Delhiite," I said teasingly as I had just got the upper hand over him. By the way, I was badly pinched by that kiss over the phone.

"And you are happy with the verdict because Dhoni speaks the same regional language as that of yours." He retorted.

"Now where did that come from?" I asked getting irritated by his witty reply.

"I just borrowed your logic." He replied calmly.

"You are too much. You never accept your defeat. You think you are invincible." I said.

"So you want to defeat me. Okay, you are competing with me." He started playing around me by saying that.

"No, not at all. Have I lost my mind?" I replied managing the situation.

"Let's open another bottle of beer?" I added, shifting from argument to alcohol.

That was the fifth and the last bottle of beer, which meant we had to share it if we both were going to consume it. But Kabeer generously dedicated the entire bottle to me as a reward for India's grand victory plus my acceptance of night stay at DENCITY on his request. Though the bottle now totally belonged to me, yet he too, in between, took swigs of the content inside it. Anshu was totally unaware of the mess we had created in the hall as the pills made him sleep soundly in his room. Kabeer didn't smoke, as far as I knew but as he offered the last bottle entirely to me, in order to accompany me in the intoxication, he borrowed Anshu's cigarette case without his permission and in fact without his knowledge. Well, real friendship doesn't believe in fulfilling the civil and informative criteria of formality.

"Are you regular into it?"I asked seeing him fagging.

"Honestly, this is the second attempt." He replied emitting the fume.

"And what's with Radhika?" I asked audaciously.

"She doesn't smoke, I guess. Does she?" He replied in a serious tone and then snickered.

"Be serious," I said getting irked easily.

"I really am. She seriously doesn't smoke." He repeated the previous answer, finding it very funny.

"Fine, don't tell. I'll not ask you anymore." I sulked as if I was his girlfriend.

"Don't get upset, you angry monster. Ask whatever you want to." He said being generous to me again.

My anger did the trick for me or Kabeer's over happiness or alcohol inside us, or probably all of them.

"I smell that there is something going on between you and her. Is it?" I tried to make the sum.

"As in?" he reduced the size of a cigarette into a stub in almost no time and then started playing around again.

"As in, you know... something, something," I replied in his fashion.

"Can't say, exactly," He replied, unsure.

"Meaning?" I asked.

"Bro, it's no rocket science to understand what she feels for me but it really is one to understand my perspective." His explanation gave birth to another question.

"And what is yours, actually?" I asked in order to understand.

"Leave, *na*. It doesn't count anyways." He said sounding hopeless and looked away from me.

"Kabeer, now you are running away from your feelings." I sounded like some typical Love *guru*, even to myself.

"It's not about running away or chasing them. Basically, it doesn't validate my personality, precisely." He said, trying to evade the matter.

"I know you are gay. Even I knew this since the beginning. But don't worry it's legal nowadays." I gave the final verdict.

"Oh really, so now that you have finally understood my sexual orientation, can I ask you to be mine forever?" He shifted towards me proposed to me, apparently finding me compatible.

He instantly implemented my suggestion on me and left me dumbfounded. I was very sure that he must be kidding but still for some unknown reasons, it took me a lot of time and a hell lot of the strength to react normally to his casual statement

"No, I am not born that way." I tried to swallow my saliva and replied.

"Me neither," He said and cackled, shifting back to his position.

I was scared abominably for one moment. If he hadn't introduced me quickly with the fact of the matter, I probably would've woken Anshu up as a safety measure. I even thought of escaping from there. I was literally shaken even after all the alcohol. I had imagined the unspeakable in those 60 odd seconds and when I am saying 60 seconds instead of 1 minute, one himself can imagine how dreadful it would have been for me to live with. I mean not having Radhika in my life ever was a completely different and tractable thing for me than being with Kabeer as a couple for eternity. I would always have preferred to be in mourning if Radhika and I couldn't make it together but I never even imagined of Kabeer as a substitute or consoling partner, either. Though I had had no girlfriend in my entire spent life, yet that didn't mean I was ready to compromise. My family was still there like most of the Indians have, as the last ray of hope to get a girl for losers like me. Needle in the haystack has no meaning for Indian parents when it comes to spotting a match for their own child or of anyone in the clan. I haven't figured it out yet, that as parents whether it's their hobby or they are purely blessed with some special power by God but whatever it is, they always love to act as a match-maker and anyhow find a so-called suitable match (of opposite sex) in the end.

For a moment, Almighty took my breath away. But I will always be in debt to thee on my renaissance. Kabeer was really the devil.

"Yeah, I do have feelings for her." He said interrupting my thought process.

I shook my head to blur the visualizations I recently went through. He lit up another stick and started proceedings somewhat like Sherlock Holmes.

"I started liking her since the beginning. Well, she herself is likable and adorable. A fellow, one feels lucky and fun to be around. She is an antique-piece, absolutely one of her kind. A lady of value and wisdom, I must say. And they say 'Beauty is the wisdom of a woman', but in her case, beauty and wisdom both are different, considerable and meaningful. She is beautiful as hell, which could make anyone fall on their knees for her, literally anyone. Her eyes, her hair, her grace, everything is so archetype to make anyone fall at her appearance itself. And *yet*, she is single. Do you know, why? Because she is much more than just an eye-candy figure as she possesses a lovely heart, a heart of gold full of bravery and compassion at the same time. Despite some big and heart-wrenching losses, she has no grudges and grievances towards life. All in all, she is a gutsy girl with a heart full of love, who always believes in loving unconditionally. And she is someone you can always find standing by you, no matter from which phase of life you are walking through. She is that rumour which everybody wishes to turn true for them. But above all, I have profuse respect for her in my heart because of her well-determined character. I know she loves me and wants to be with me forever by forming an unbreakable and heavenly alliance and I intuit that she is very well aware of the fact that I know those feelings of her for me but for some strange reason, I tend to shy away from all these things. And that is something really unique about her as my abstruseness didn't make her turn to some other guy, yet she was and is flooded with such sort of proposals from others every now and then. But that is the proof of her wisdom and character, which has made it irresistible for me to keep her away from me. Her determination also gives an illusion of stubbornness which is actually not real, it has kept me in fear of losing my soul to her. I still have that fear."

The flow, with which Kabeer was going, seemed that he could write an entire book on her but his over 5 minutes speech didn't solve my query either. But then, before I could ask him another question, he himself commenced again. Alcohol at times is not that bad, I realized.

"Well, she looks beauteous all the time but that day, on her birthday she was looking exceptional, just as an epitome of elegance. I am damn sure you would also have noticed her. Her long peach coloured *Anarkali* suit, which was almost an entire long dress, had totally adorned her beauty . And it's not that I haven't seen her in that traditional avatar earlier but that day she was looking as beautiful as a bride. That tuft of natural light-brown hair of hers, with some deliberate curls towards the bottom and a maroon color, tiny bindi on her forehead had literally transformed her into an angel. In fact, the drunken angel was looking much cuter in her actions. And when she pulled me across her....."

I fell asleep on the roof that night and therefore I thought that was how the party ended. But no, there was something more to it. Kabeer was going to reveal something which I was totally unaware of. My heart started beating faster as he took a pause to catch his own breath during narration. Probably, it had already sensed that he was going to reveal something which I deliberately wanted to listen but actually, shouldn't. That was an alarm from the heart but my mind had different plans. And therefore my mouth operated accordingly as my mind instructed.

"What happened after that Kabeer, when she pulled you across?" I asked trying not to express my actual feelings.

"I was that much close to her, Vishu." He replied bringing his index finger and thumb closer to each other.

The blood in my heart started pumping faster. My heart went on 2X beating mode per minute but I somehow managed to remain silent and inexpressive while he continued.

"Though it was pitch-dark there on the roof, yet I could see her face clearly. Her kohl applied eyes were stuck to mine and became much wider as I continuously kept looking into them. With complete innocence, her elongated square shaped face was looking at me and I was able to feel the warmth of her bouncy breath, which were finding their destination on my cheeks. But sooner, the compressed area around us used all the possible fresh Oxygen available nearby, forced her to breathe, also through the mouth and in the process, the light green nerves at her neck were stressed and started peeping out of her fair complexioned skin. I don't know whether it was some perfume or her natural body fragrance, but I still have the feel of it. I was continuously looking at her with the utmost 'dumbassdom'. And then suddenly with an unconventional gust at an unexpected time, a curl came onto her eye. My reflexes instantly guided my finger to push it away and her reflexes accordingly, made her shut both the eyes. As she was already tugging my t-shirt firmly with both her hands, I moved an inch nearer to her and she started shivering. Her heartbeats became so loud, that for a second, I actually mistook them for mine. She kept her eyes closed in anticipation and I started exploring her captivating face and eventually traced a tiny mole right below her lower lip on the extreme right, which got me hypnotized for a few seconds. I again saw her face completely. It was flawless. I haven't witnessed anything so beautiful ever at such marginal distance. She is too damn beautiful."

Kabeer stopped himself but I hadn't. The restiveness that arose inside me now both, wanted and needed to listen to the complete story.

"And then?" I asked with restlessness.

"I wrapped her in my arms. She too loosened her grasp over my apparel and completely surrendered herself to me. The way she embraced me, I could easily reckon that she must be habitual of a big teddy to sleep with. She was soft like silk and was totally cosy. I whispered something into her ear but she was reaction-less. I, then again, blew some air in her right ear and she grabbed me firmly. She was in complete solace and as I didn't feel like breaking her continuity, so I let her stay in it."

The detailed explanation of everything Kabeer gave about Radhika was the authentication of 'what has been going on in Kabeer's mind for last few days'. It wasn't a million dollar question but it arrived along with the millions of questions in my tiny mind.

"Didn't you kiss her?" I asked as I couldn't think of that action not performed between them.

"Nope," He replied with an innocent smile.

"So she surely would've kissed you?" I asked the same question trying to be funny, just to assure myself again.

"Sorry, but the answer is again the same i.e. 'NO'." He replied.

"Are you kidding?" I said as I wasn't satisfied with the answer. It was really unbelievable to hear that after so much drama.

"Are you feeling so?" he replied in a question.

"But why so?" I kept looking for an answer.

"I have a girlfriend." He whispered and stood up.

*

It was 3:00 in the morning when Kabeer apprised me with that title of his new untold story and went to the washroom. I too went after him but the latest-fed information in my brain was unable to keep my mind relaxed. While separating real and imaginary parts of the equation and focusing more on the imaginary ones as I had no idea of what the reality was up to, my eyes coincidentally peeped out through the ventilator of the washroom. It was still dark outside, though a new day had already started technically. I instantly called my mission of peeing and pondering off and sprinted to the hall. I used to be afraid of the dark. I still am.

Kabeer directed me towards his room as he came out of the kitchen holding a flask of water. His body language was telling that he wanted us to sleep. I silently went to the room followed by him. Luckily, he didn't see me running and I too didn't want him to know that darkness rips me up.

Darkness reminded me of his girlfriend, who was either invisible or otherwise hidden in some kind of darkness. Now here I got a solid point and that bloke wanted me to sleep. Well, she couldn't be invisible. Being a student of science and technology, at least I wasn't supposed to believe that. So basically he had a girlfriend in hiding. Correction... he had hidden his girlfriend from us for almost 4 years. He neither revealed about her by himself nor hinted anything like it ever. Was he cooking up some fake story again in order to get rid of my unnecessary questions? Was he just playing around? If no, then how come he made it possible to not open up about her any time? Was she really invisible? Was he also some wandering spirit or some RAW or ISI agent? Was he on some coveted mission?

"Some people find it hard to believe and some can't even afford to believe it." I was particularly the former type when it came to believing Kabeer. No, I am not saying that I didn't count on him. In fact, he was the only person for whom I would've gotten ready to defy even the law of gravity if he had ever asked me to do so. But whenever he used to introduce to me a new story or incidences about anything, I always found it impossible to reckon its actuality. I, many times, became a prey of his pranks, so it was more like once bitten, twice shy. I knew very well how good he was at cooking and faking stories and one never got to know until the end, if he was really sharing his experience or playing some prank as he was a natural prankster. At the same time the truth of the matter is, real incidences witnessed by one, are somewhere more responsible for inspiring him to think out of the box. And if he wasn't lying, then it really was big news for me. He already possessing a girlfriend could serve my purpose without a hitch as Radhika would probably leave craving for him, after knowing that. YEAH! It wasn't going to prove at all that I was the best and second to none but now getting Radhika had become a higher priority. Priorities change according to the needs and people change according to their priorities. It was a kind of positive assurance and I was now more hopeful that she wouldn't reject my proposal.

But as of now, Kabeer's girlfriend had arisen more interest in me rather than mine-in-process. He had already tried to evade the discussion a bit as his alcohol and happiness level, both had come down because of our chit-chatting of over 2 hours at a stretch. However it wasn't a mindless banter until now, he just spoke his heart all the way and when heart speaks up, nothing can match to its oratory. I really wanted to hear the prequel of that story and hence my consistent insistence and 'crave for more' did the trick, finally.

"Vishu, we are already entered into a new day and the story is really very long. I know I am sounding quite filmy but that is the only truth." Kabeer kept delaying rather than commencing.

"No issue brother, I'll extend my already extended stay over here," I replied back to him in his typical way, defying that Radhika was not the only person considered to be determined and stubborn (as he mentioned).

****

CHAPTER 12

"THE LONG STORY (OF KABEER BHAAGWAT)"

DEHRADUN,

CAPITAL OF UTTARAKHAND – A hilly area known best for its natural resources and IMA (INDIAN MILITARY ACADEMY).

"My father Gokul Bhaagwat was a non-commissioned officer, who served for the Indian army and died for the motherland. Before his last posting at Jammu & Kashmir, he was posted at IMA Dehradun, as an integral part of the recruitment and training cell of the Gentleman cadet. I was almost a crawling baby when we stepped in the land of deities for the first time. My one and only elder sibling Meera was 5 years old then. And I am 4 years younger than her, quite young that time. After completing his tenure of 5 years at IMA Dehradun, my father got posted at Jammu & Kashmir. Because of some unforeseen conditions and our schooling, we

somehow ended up settling down in Dehradun itself and as we were already residing in the government allotted quarter, it was more of a wise decision to stay there. But within a year of posting at J&K, we lost the head of our family to terrorism. He sacrificed himself fighting against militants at KUPWARA, J&K.

Ours was a small family of 4, which further got reduced to 3, the two out of which were minor, then. The entire burden of the family shifted to a lady who was just of 28 years. I wouldn't call her as a woman because I don't think she, then, was mature enough to be called one. The lady's name was Vanita, which means a graceful lady. Though she wasn't educated enough on paper, yet she sought enough knowledge and wisdom through experiences of life, at a very early age. William Shakespeare once wrote an entire book titled as "What's in the name?" And that graceful lady taught me that, "Your name could be meaningless, but your life shouldn't be".

Life didn't seem easy for her but she was still trying her best to lead it from the front for her two children, Meera and Kabeer. One was her expectation and other was hope."

She wisely purchased a small apartment from most of the funds and remuneration, which she received from the government against losing her husband as the government housing facility got terminated soon. The pension, she was receiving on her husband's behalf turned into a dwarf as the children started maturing. From food to schooling, the expenses started inclining.

Raising additional fund was the need of the time. Eventually, Vanita started a small cafeteria by renting a shop where beverages and snacks were provided. Though it wasn't enough to generate a hefty amount instantly yet it was a small step towards something. They say, 'A lone soldier cannot win a war,' but some battles are meant to be fought alone.

Meera was in her early teens when she started assisting her mother. After her school, she used to sit at the shop. Also, she took over the charge of looking after the home and her younger brother. Gradually, the soldier got her subordinate as well as courage. Parallelly, with God's grace, their cafeteria became a hit among locals and tourists, both and the soldier with her subordinate started conquering kingdoms along with hearts.

The Cafeteria turned into a Restaurant after a continuous and steadfast effort of 5 years and a 28 years old lady became 33 years old woman in exchange for just 5 years. The 5 years which could've been spent luxuriously if her husband was alive, were turned into the 5 years of almost poverty, sorrow, isolation and stress for her. But she didn't give up. She wasn't meant for giving up. After all, she was an Army man's wife. Well, it doesn't matter at all if her husband was an Army man or a civilian. What matters was the courage and determination she displayed throughout the journey in which she herself was the navigator as well as the passenger. She was a woman of mettle. Indeed, a woman of values and principles who had respect for herself and fear of her soul.

Meera and Kabeer grew up all too soon, especially the former one. Meera, after completing her schooling, went to Nainital for pursuing a degree in computer administration as she got admission in a government recognized university over there. It was a 3 years course and coincidentally she, in her last academic year, fell in love with a boy who was pursuing masters in the same course from the same college.

Kabeer who had grown up seeing her mother and sister sacrificing a lot for everything became quite mature beyond his age. And as he was good at grasping skills quickly, he became better as a performer, a performer who seldom commits any mistake and mostly performs at par. He himself became the talk of the town until he reached the senior secondary level of schooling. Besides his eye candy looks, his all-rounder activity in every department of schooling from academics to sports made him quite popular, especially among the lassies. And naturally, with age, he too fell for a girl, who also was in love with him. They emerged as the complimenting couple as they were totally dedicated towards their relationship. Within barely a period of 1 year, their bond went much stronger and deeper and they kept continuing it until destiny played its part and put them all in an awkward situation.

Meera told her mother about her relationship with Raaghav, who happened to belong to a minority community. The boy, was all good, well-cultured and born to a well to do family but Meera's mom was not pleased with that association of two different communities and hence didn't give a nod of approval to them. With lots of unconvincing arguments, unavoidable tortures and unending stress on a daily basis, nobody reached to any definitive decision of what should be actually done to win over the other.

With a sudden rise of such unforeseen situations, Meera's mom Vanita started living in fear and despair. The entire values and the principles, she had been teaching to her children for years, suddenly started sounding hollow to her. She started feeling like she had reached nowhere after trudging all over the years, which led her to believe that her diligence, sacrifices, worship, luck, everything fell to pieces. Her children made her weak and her over-thinking made her unwell.

Kabeer was the only unbiased witness of all that melodramatic chaos happening over there. From bad to worse, he travelled that whole journey of free fall along with his mother as a co-passenger, as Meera had already gone back to college for her finals. Going back to college was just a social formality for her to dissociate herself from home while in actuality, the two females of the house, had already gone miles away in the opposite direction like two parallel lines maintaining a symmetrical and continuous gap of respective notions. Kabeer was the only person left who could lessen the distance between the soldier and her darling subordinate. He needed to act like a bridge, so that the two parallel lines, which once used to completely overlap each other, could manage to touch each other again but not intersect.

Someone was needed to come forward and carry the burden on his shoulder, so that soldier and subordinate would nullify their differences and reform their kingdom into an empire. And deep down, Kabeer got himself ready to be the bull beneath that earth.

Being constantly with the mother, he nursed her with all the love and care because of which, mother soon showed speedy recovery. And afterward, Kabeer tried a lot to convince her on Meera's marriage proposal but the mother was now much unsure as what she saw of her daughter's latest rebellious behaviour. He really wanted to make peace with their lives but he couldn't afford to display any sign of bias for either of the two. He knew, like his mother, his sister had sacrificed a lot to make the conditions liveable for the clan. And all in all, it was her maiden-demand for herself among all over the years as she actually got damn serious about that relationship and that was why she argued so bluntly with her mother for the first time in her entire spent life. Meera was like the second mother to Kabeer and he couldn't bear the pain of losing any of his mothers. So he eventually decided to make everything fine and dandy between the two, no matter what it cost him.

Kabeer who recently experienced everything so closely about the family's breakup, which caused his mom to suffer from illness, had no doubt left in his mind to decide what to do. It was no rocket science for him to understand that first of all he had to call his relationship off with his beloved girlfriend (about whom, his family wasn't aware of, either). And as he had also taken the responsibility of convincing his mother for Meera's choice, so he further decided to give up on his lifelong dream of being an Army man. Kabeer who was very fond of soldiers and patriotism, always wanted to be a defence personnel like his father, but his mother never supported him for it ever since she lost her husband. She knew how much Kabeer loved and was passionate for the army and hence he used it finally as a tool by promising his mother on not thinking of joining the army if she would consider Meera's choice for marriage.

Well, soldier, after all, was a mother, a mother of two brave-hearts. Meera, the subordinate, had always supported her mother in every step of life, ever since she came into senses. The soldier mother just wanted to see her daughter happy. She became extra protective towards the children after losing her husband, which was allowed and quite natural. Her concern was to just choose best of both worlds for her offspring so that they would never have to suffer even by mistake. Yes, she was asking for too much from the almighty but she was asking for her children, with the utmost selflessness. And when Kabeer initiated the gelling process of the family, she managed to restore her faith in her children and realized that the kids had finally grown up, who actually valued the family beyond all their personal priorities. Kabeer who appeared, one week later as the third semester began in the college, was actually busy in his sister's marriage.

But in the process of finding a way to bind his family together, the path he chose for himself was impassable. And the biggest irony was he himself was his pioneer as he didn't reveal to anyone about his coveted mission. The promise was a sheer bet. And he had deliberately challenged himself. The hope he raised again in their mother, had then also become an expectation to him from himself. And he kept his promise. Though he received a lot of criticism from everyone who used to know about his relationship yet he didn't utter a single word either in explanation or in retortion. He coped with everything, whatever came in his path...the love, the pain, and the unending suffering.

Meanwhile, the girl, whom he was in a relationship with, tried a lot to contact him and bring him back but he didn't let himself breach his promise, made to himself. He just cut himself off everything which was anyhow linked to her. The motive of joining the college in Delhi was the same. He, probably, was much harsh at himself as compared to life. And hitting the last nail in the coffin, he made things look like he deliberately cheated on her so that she could start hating him all from her heart and try to move on. Things worked according to his plan and she gave up on him, finally. She was left without any alternative.

Success doesn't mean winning always, sometimes losing intentionally, is kind of one. Kabeer redefined the meaning of success, that particular day. He intentionally chose to lose, to cry, to suffer and to trade his innocence. His logic of breaking up with her without any innuendo was to not interfere ever in her life, anyhow. He was sure that she would have neither let him go nor given up herself if he would've chosen to apprise her with the exact reason. Though she acted at no fault of hers yet she got tormented because of him. But Pain makes one stronger than that he ever thought of, he would be too.

Kabeer was never able to forgive himself for that option-less but menacing decision, though he knew he had to go through anguish, no matter either which way he would've chosen. Kabeer hurt a pure heart for no reason but he intentionally killed his. He afterward, never passed a day without thinking of her and sobbing for her in his loneliness. He always prayed and hoped for her happiness and betterment while he himself lived all those years in guilt, after leaving her. He chose to live so that he could punish himself until the day of reckoning. And moreover, it isn't extreme if it doesn't last longer than one.

Meanwhile, at the family end, things got contently settled with progressing time. Meera and Raaghav are leading their life blissfully. Vanita the soldier, and mother has again made herself busy with her Restaurant. And everyone's favourite Kabeer is also happy with his friends and family. After all, they are his Life. But he has a wish... just a single one. He only wants to seek forgiveness from that girl, who once was his girlfriend. I know he doesn't deserve it at all still, he is hopeful that... One fine day, life will pay all her debts.

****

CHAPTER 13

"I HAVE A GIRLFRIEND TO I ONCE HAD A GIRLFRIEND"

Kabeer, an expert in cooking up real-time stories, actually had a story for real, a story of his own life, the brutal one. It was completely unbelievable for me, something which was exceptionally hard to digest.

Someone who had an image of being the BOY-NEXT-DOOR was actually a boy who is barely found next doors. He, who himself invented him that way, was a sheer discovery for me. A smile can cover up so many things, I realized it then. And like his smile, his story was much more killing. The visuals of last 4 years I spent with him, suddenly took a random start in my mind. The day he received slaps on his face from the senior student to the day the same face got a kiss from Radhika, he was all in guilt for a decision he took in order to make almost everything exquisite. YEAH! No one forced him to do any such thing but no one served the purpose either.

ALAS! He had always been burning with the flame of guilt, but he neither repented his decision nor let himself breach the promise he had made to himself. Instead, he let himself burn with the flame of compassion and lit up the darkness of callowness around him. Illuminating my life was entirely his trait. I was able to relate to the pain and agony he had gone through but what I was unable to reckon, was the expanse.

Life sometimes becomes unfair... but it goes on. Kabeer struggled but survived and tried again to redefine his life, after coming to Delhi. He was never a coward because cowards run away from situations. They never think of even stepping out of their comfort zone and hence end up in screwing their relationships for their own selfishness. But he saved too many relationships, sacrificing his own and afterward confronted everything facing it without complaining about it and that too, alone. He made every possible adjustment and at times, even impossible ones too.

"Don't think too much. It all happened way back, now I am much stable." Kabeer tapped my shoulder as he sensed my long but meaningful silence.

"Do you still love her?" I curiously asked to know his perception of his present status.

"LOVE," He pronounced the word after me and brooded.

"Yes, love for her," I asked again.

"I never get to understand the exact definition of this word and I guess, I never will. But yes, I've missed her a lot over the years," he said as he got off the bed and proceeded towards the hall.

He, after reaching there, opened the door of the hall which he bolted up at night or morning. Dawn had broken. I could see it from the room. The light rays, which were knocking at the door earlier, had entered into the hall as the door was opened. I too stepped out of the bed and came to the hall, following him. He was standing quite normally in the balcony, attached to the hall and watched the Delhi dawn-break. I tiptoed to him.

"What are you doing here, bro?" I asked putting my hand around his shoulder.

"Vitamin D," he replied signalling towards the sun and smiled looking at me.

"And what about vitamin T (tea), don't you need that?" I said kneading softly at his shoulder muscles.

He closed his eyes as he felt a bit relaxed and then indicated to me with his hand to continue it. I, without saying anything, obeyed him.

"Ah! Heaven, I really owe you a cup of vitamin T, right now." He said after a while, stopping my hands.

"Sure, why not?" I replied happily.

Within the next 5 minutes, Kabeer and I were walking down the road to a park nearby, dressed up in the same shorts and tee shirts we were wearing since last night. It was past 5:45 am when we left DENCITY. The road was totally vacant unlike daytime and honestly, I didn't remember a single day when I had woken up before the 7'o clock in Delhi. So it was my nascent experience of how Delhi looked at sunrise, though the sun had almost come out of its shed completely. Birds had also taken off from their shelters and a few people had already come on the promenade, like us. A new ray of hope had commenced and honestly, I liked that exclusive view of silent Delhi, which rest of the time, was not the same. We reached the park sooner but avoided entering it. The park was rectangular in shape and was enclosed by a 3-4 feet cemented wall upon which iron railings were fixed. Kabeer set our route to the tea kiosk, which was right next to the park, almost like a 4X4 cubicle. Contrary to its size, it was the centre of attraction for the early birds. A fixed cemented bench placed in front of it was already occupied by customers. Two cups tea and a black (cigarette), Kabeer ordered to the vendor and paid for it. We received our order as it got served faster than ROGER FEDERER's ace and then moved some 20-25 steps back along with the fence of the park. Kabeer who had already lit up was shuffling his fag alternatively with the sip of tea. I dont know if he was smoking it correctly or not but surely he was enjoying holding it between his fingers. We both were peeping inside the park from outside while consuming our vitamin T. Not sure about Kabeer, but I had already started checking the girls out who were jogging inside the park, wearing yoga pants and shorts. In the middle of the park, there were few kids playing cricket. I looked at Kabeer. He was probably concentrating on their game, although he wasn't shying away from giving a glance to the girls as they kept obstructing his direct line of sight while running. Kabeer, girls and cricket, all at the same place automatically brought something into my notice which was quite unusual. Well, last night was itself an example of unusualness. It was unusual also because I noticed it. I wanted to resist myself from asking but I couldn't. I seriously didn't want him to dwell on the past again but I couldn't help it.

"Don't you think you are the unsung hero, somewhat like Gautam Gambhir of yesterday's match?" I asked Kabeer referring to his life's tragic story.

"*Haan*? Did you say something to me?" He replied a few seconds later, totally concentrating on the game, not looking at me.

I repeated my question.

"Oh! I think that's my mom." He replied quite easily, tried looking towards me but then didn't.

"So you must be the skipper?" I said as if there were only two options available, like in a coin.

"That's Meera suitably. She has always backed up our clan's priorities and kept us motivated. And also she fought for her love and eventually achieved it too." he replied in an answer along with the justification.

"But it was you who made their marriage possible. Isn't it?" I kept distracting him with my arguments, which were sheer logic, just to know how he perceived himself as.

He turned towards me this time. I looked at the kids.

Their game was still on which meant he deliberately did so. Probably he wanted me to shut my mouth.

"See Vishu, Family is just like a team and vice versa, in which everyone has a role to play. And I never mind being the skipper or the 12th man of this team, as far as my team is happy and winning. And particularly in my situation, I felt that I could perform better that way, so I executed like that. I strongly felt that I could strengthen this Bhaagwat clan by doing what I did. A family always needs a resilient force which could keep them hopeful and motivated in their rainy days. That time, I became that force. After all, Family is a team gifted by nature, in which individual's performance doesn't matter the way team performance does. And seriously for me, recognizance is not as important as the togetherness and happiness of my family." He replied with conviction.

Kabeer was really a hard-hitter and a family man in a true sense.

"Didn't you ever try to contact her anytime?" I asked trying to explore his vision with my curiosity.

"Actually I had thought of not interfering in her life ever but then I did. Though I don't have her contact number yet I have been sending messages to wish on her birthday through FACEBOOK for last two years. But she is quite unresponsive. And it's thoroughly justified. I screwed up her life for my selfishness. I deliberately created a tough time for her and then left her alone in it. So, that much is allowed from her side. But you know Vishu, I beseechingly want to see her happy anyhow. All I want for me is an opportunity to say Sorry once or you can say I am patiently trying to make an opportunity by sending those birthday messages to her." He said while staring at the paper cup he was holding.

"There might be many occasions when the character hidden within us feels like changing. It tempts to do so, maybe for good or bad. But I realized there are two definite occasions when it does change for sure. First, when love steps in one's life and second when it walks out. And coincidentally, I have gone through both." He added further and kept continuing.

"And now, I've become quite open to challenges. Even, I myself tried many times, to challenge me. Something inside me, has died, probably some fear. There was a time when I started feeling unsure over my adequacies. I used to feel as if I was a loser. The soul inside me kept yelling about my innocence, but situations against me were proving me fugitive. Situations vaulted me firmly. But I knew I was on some test. And therefore I never let the fire inside me, to turn into animosity. I happened to cope with those situations and Nature, in return, gifted me friends like you, Anshu, Sid, Lucky, and Radhika. I am truly grateful to GOD." He paused as he thanked God.

"You know that day when I cried, I actually felt some kind of déjà vu. It was Radhika's birthday. She was in all good mood and I spoilt everything like I did in my past. It offended me thoroughly and then when she hugged me even after my stupidity, I couldn't control myself. I felt relieved. Relieved from the guilt that was nagging me constantly for the last 4 years. I always wanted to cry on my ex's shoulder but eventually, Radhika came to rescue me a tad from my past." He ended the elaboration of his perception on a hopeful note.

"But Kabeer, you could've told everything to your mother and who knows, if she would also get convinced for her too?" I asked again.

"You remember I went to Bhopal for Army SSB interview in the second year of the college. It was my mom, who insisted me to fill that application form and posted it, defying her own Do's and Don'ts. She, who always used to scold me whenever I discussed on that topic, had herself taken that initiative for me. Yes, her change of mind was possibly because she saw me sacrificing my dream to make that of Meera's, possible. But it is also true that no parents could afford to lose their offspring anyhow." He tried to explain me parenting concept rather than answering what I had asked him.

"See, there were some real possible chances for you, if only you would've revealed your reality to her." I indirectly asked him the same question citing his statement.

"Yeah, maybe she would've gotten convinced and all but I wasn't in the state of taking any possible risk with her. I was there, when she hit rock-bottom and she had almost killed herself by over-thinking. She even stopped going to the restaurant. We had nothing to talk about. I used to fumble as to what to say. She used to get out of the bed only to cook for me and she herself stopped eating, which made her look somewhat haggard. That happened for 7 continuous days. It literally became a house of the dead. I prayed a lot to God for my mom's wellness and in return, I was ready to do anything. I couldn't see her dying, Vishu. She means everything to me. I couldn't take her to the same situation again, where she was been to earlier. I just couldn't." He crushed the paper cup within his fist as he signed off.

Kabeer who hitherto, was trying to show he was unaffected, eventually broke down abominably. He was absolutely innocent but his innocence didn't work in his favour. Well, greatness does come with a price but Kabeer also didn't buy it. Instead, he waived its price off with his sacrifices. He totally deserved it and ultimately he managed to earn it too. His girlfriend might not accept it though, as she had done no wrong but would've got punished as well as affected emotionally, by Kabeer's solo decision of separation. She must have her version of the story and how did she deal with life afterward, for sure. She even might've perceived him as gutless and selfish. But then, every mortal thing in this Universe is selfish. 'HOW MUCH' doesn't matter much the way 'WHY' counts.

I hugged Kabeer as tightly as I could. I desperately wanted to hug him ever since I heard the complete story. And then, he himself blessed me with that auspicious opportunity of embosoming him. I rubbed his back gently. My ideal was in my arms. And Ideals are someone you always look up to and not to compete tyrannically with.

****

CHAPTER 14

"THE STUPID CUPID"

A lot had happened over that night, something which was sheerly unprecedented.

- India lifted the Cricket world cup again after 28 years.

- Kabeer for the first time in 4 years, divulged his big hush-hush to anyone.

- I finally realized my oversight.

Kabeer had always been an ocean of inspiration for me but now my respect towards him reached its apogee. It was purely my stupidity to constantly try on competing with a person, who had always been abetting toward me. I wanted to go beyond him because he made me believe that I could, otherwise I, very well knew where I stood in my initial days of college. That was the wallop of his friendship.

I honestly had nothing to do with his story but it certainly touched the strings of my heart and melted those emotions which were somehow, frozen for no reason.

A best friend, very well, knows how bad an actor the other one is. And I was not the one who deserved to be known as BEST FRIEND. That, 'SO-CALLED-BEST-FRIEND' was probably invented for me, I guessed. I, on my own, never got to know about Kabeer's ineffable pain behind his beautiful smile. But now was high time for me to prove my brotherhood to him. Radhika, whom I wanted to acquire just to humiliate him, obviously because of my folly, was the best way of my reconciliation with him. And their tailor-made closeness with each other was the icing on the cake to my gentle and latest expedition.

I was determined for a noble cause like never before. I hoped I could make it.

*

Radhika took out a serviette from the denim handbag and wiped her tears off. Now that's some pretty awkward situation to handle in a public place where one of the two persons, starts shedding tears and the situation tends to become weirdest when the crying person is a girl but not your girlfriend. You aren't left with much options then.

"Radhika, we are in the canteen." I said while reminding her of the people around.

She didn't care of what I murmured and continued her tear-show unaffected of the students present there.

Radhika and I were in the canteen when I narrated to her, the entire story of Kabeer's past. Well, I always wanted to tell her the big secret ever since I got to know it. She was totally dumbstruck like I was when Kabeer shared it with me. My motive of narration to her was simple and straight. Kabeer also had feelings for her and the reason behind not disclosing them was that unbelievable story. I wanted her to be aware of everything, what he had gone through of and how he developed his perception. Though she had already shown whatever her heart got for him, yet it would be a completely different approach to convince him after knowing about his past. And as per my expectation, the love for Kabeer inside her heart was ready to explode as she got to know one more different side of him. My narration over his past had coincidentally set her heart on. She eventually got the impeccable reason and the situation to express her love to him through words. And I was more than happy to be the CUPID in their love story.

"Vishu, let's go. I need to meet him right now." She said while rearranging her handbag which she messed up while taking out that wipe.

"Let me finish this samosa," I replied, looking for that mole below her lower lip (which Kabeer got to discover on her face).

A minute almost negligible black spot was all I found after giving much stress to my eyes. Well, I still wasn't sure if he was talking about it or some other one. It already took me a hell of a lot of concentration to find that one only, on that really extremely flawless and spotless face, which by the way, couldn't hypnotize me at all. After all, it's solely the matter of feelings which can make you imagine any unreal thing to be real and Kabeer did have those 'ANYTHING-FOR-YOU' feelings for her.

"Be quick na, what are you thinking?" She, after giving me a hurried glance, said and got busy in her handbag setting.

"Just a minute, by the way, what will you say to him?" I mumbled, making that rest of the more than half of the samosa as my last bite.

I was a glutton and I still am. You can keep feeding me and I'll never ask you to stop. Offer me a plate of samosa with a coke and I could give my ATM card along with its pin, even to a stranger. Though I then used to be completely bankrupt.

"Vishu, I am thinking of something. We can execute it if you do me a favor." She asked me for assistance.

"Sure. Say what I need to do." I replied while gulping down what I chewed.

"It's quite filmy and weird but you'll have to shoot a video on your cell phone as I propose to him." She said shy.

Well, weird things make memories and doing such stuff for someone, need no words to explain, that how much one loves them. Kabeer was that lucky bastard and Radhika, one more time, won my heart. She really was the exemplification of the 'Girlfriend' community. I automatically was ready for it.

"But Radhika, I have one more thing to tell you," I said.

"Regarding Kabeer?" She replied as she stood up.

"Regarding me," I said.

"Tell me, then." She said.

"No not like this. It will take me time to explain." I acquainted her with a time consumption clause.

"Then surely after my big performance, I need to focus on it right now." She said trying to look much cuter than what she actually was.

*

"ECE 3RD YEAR". It was the first room right next to the stairs, on the second floor of the college building. The second floor was entirely designated to the 3rd year batch which comprises of all the courses offered by the college. Similarly the third and the first floor were designated for 4th and 2nd-year batches respectively. There was a different building for the first-year batch, in order to keep them away from the senior batches so as to avoid any possible chances of ragging.

We happened to see Kabeer from a distance on the second floor while climbing stairs en route our classroom on the third floor. Radhika was leading and I was the follower. Her walking speed was clearly indicating her impulsiveness and impatience. She, on spotting him with 3rd-year students, was diverted from her scheduled route and moved towards the new destination. I like the coaches of a train followed the engine. He was sitting on a desk in the middle, keeping his feet over the chair, and to his opposite, a semi-circle was formed by some 8-10 students whom the classroom belonged to. Right opposite to him, Aditi was sitting on the chair facing him. Kabeer probably was sharing his valuable experience or might be narrating some real or interesting cooked up story by him to the young brigade. Well, he was quite popular among juniors and they too were immensely fond of him. Seeing Aditi with Kabeer automatically reduced Radhika's excitement level. At least I felt so. Still, she entered the room without cutting off her pre-scheduled plan. She had already instructed me to stay outside with my cell phone active on video mode as she was going to bring him outside.

"What's up, guys? No class to attend right now." She enquired the juniors after greeting them back as they wished her.

"Why not, see I am here to teach them?" Kabeer replied on their behalf.

The classroom filled with the sound of laughter.

"Kabeer sir, I too have a doubt to clear with you. Could you please clarify it to me?" Radhika asked him for a favour while walking towards him.

"Sure Genie. You are always welcome. Come, sit here." He sweetly addressed her, tapping at the desk he was sitting upon.

"No, not here, it's too personal." She too replied frankly, without any hesitation.

"Okay, but still sit here for a moment. It's sheer fun to be with all of them." He insisted her to sit.

"Definitely but some other time, you come fast now. It's really urgent." She replied in an indirect denial.

"Go, sir, there may be some urgency." Aditi tapped at Kabeer's leg, which was resting on the chair next to her and suggested.

Kabeer probably was in no mood of budging from there but the insistence of two girls couldn't go in vain and ultimately he had to leave the classroom. He exited the room following Radhika. I was already standing in the corridor waiting for them, with my cell phone in my hand. The corridor was a tad crowded but not as much, as most of the classrooms had professors in them. I glanced at Kabeer, who was already looking at me. He with the help of hand and eye coordination, signalled me pointing towards Radhika. I nodded my head horizontally in response as if I really didn't know the answer to his curiosity. He smiled and so did I. And then I pretended as If I was doing some research work on my cell phone and got busy in it. Kabeer wasn't aware at all of the fact that I was brought intentionally there to capture a lifelong memory for him because of which, he would definitely owe me for eternity. I was ready to give my best shot and so was Radhika.

"So what is that 'too personal' thing Genie, which you want me to clarify?" He asked leaning against the corridor's boundary wall and due to which I was not falling into his line of sight directly.

"Yeah, I was thinking about our after-college life, Kabeer. I mean it will be quite different unlike now." She said looking towards me, as she wanted to confirm whether I started it or not.

My excitement level of capturing the moment was more than that of her and as I was in no mood of missing even the silliest of those, therefore I already started the job assigned to me, well in time. I indicated her to rest assured and focus on the big task.

"Yep, that surely will be." He replied showing his agreement to her statement.

"So, I want to hug you." She out of the blue demanded a hug and kept delaying her proposal-plan.

"What? Here...?" He responded in shock as he didn't believe what he heard.

"Yep right here, is there any problem in it?" she asked confidently looking into his eyes.

"Is this some sort of 'DARE'?" He replied a tad nervous, seeing her confident demanding eyes and therefore looked precisely towards me. I avoided reacting at all.

"Take it as you want but I will address it much as a 'TRUTH'." She answered him back. To me, it was not looking a bit of a love proposal. Radhika was confusing me as well as his beau-to-be.

"Truth.... ok and which is what?" Kabeer tried to find her logic which she earlier described to him as 'too personal'.

"I LOVE YOU KABEER." She finally hit the last nail in the coffin. She came to the pleasant point after a couple of twists and turns.

Kabeer didn't say a word but smiled. He smiled like a girl, who was already aware that something like that was going to happen. I honestly, didn't get if he was blushing or not but my camera was busy in capturing his each and every expression, by means of which I could coerce him anytime. I was happy as I almost got my due, to tease him forever and probably Radhika too got her much-awaited answer, the question for which she asked Kabeer right then, but always kept asking herself for a long time.

"Muaahh," She sealed the opportunity and stamped her confirmation by planting a kiss on his cheek.

She asked for a hug and did more than that. He was still smiling like an infant who doesn't know what's going around him but keeps getting the love and attention of the people around.

"I am so happy, you know." She shouted in excitement just after kissing him.

"Genie, if I am not wrong, you must be thinking of commencing a relationship with me?" Kabeer spoke with surety keeping that smile on his face.

"Yes, of course, my love, I've always fantasized about it.

But why are you asking like that?" She grabbed his hand and replied curiously.

"Honestly, I can't afford to be a part of any such relationship." He exploded a new bomb with that remark.

"What does that mean Kabeer?" She furiously asked and grasped his hand even more firmly.

"I can't commit." He replied and explained the meaning.

Kabeer, the prankster, was again playing a prank, I thought. Or had he come to know about this secret video shoot and that was why behaving like a weirdo. Anything could be possible with him and he could make anything possible for himself. I was still in the dilemma about the precise reasoning of the situation.

"Don't be rude, Kabeer." Radhika pleaded innocently.

"Believe me Genie, I am not. I am just apprising you with the truth and which is too far from your imagination. I don't possess any of the qualities of a dream boy, whom you may have fantasized of. I am not even good at relationships and more than that, you are way above me. You deserve someone better, someone who can take care of you and your dreams and that's definitely not me. I am no more than a narcissist." He said, completely underestimating himself.

"I know you very well. We'll make everything fine together." She said and kissed his hand, which she was already holding.

"Genie, you don't know anything. Please don't compel me. I beg you." he responded in a plea.

"Really, am I compelling you Kabeer? You yourself know that you love me and you are saying that I am compelling you. Kabeer, you aren't guilty of whatever happened in your life. Indeed, you saved both, lives and relationships at the cost of your happiness. You did everything selflessly with the utmost good intentions and believe me, having you as my beau lifelong will be a blessing to me. I am proud of you and I respect you more than anything. I love you, Kabeer." She caught her breath as she finished speaking.

It was really important for her to explain what she actually felt for him. She really didn't want to settle for less than what she actually deserved. And in the process of convincing him, she said something which Kabeer didn't like at all or he wasn't expecting it from her at that point of time. It was his secret story which didn't remain a secret anymore. He didn't warn me to not tell anyone about it, but nor did he indicate to announce it to the public. I, also, hadn't thought of it that way and with all the good intentions, I revealed it only to his Genie. I just wanted to be the adhesive force between their perfect blend but this time my good intentions were not enough to conquer over my earlier bad intentions. We are entitled to 'either receive an honour or pay for our sin' on behalf of our respective intentions and presentations, but totally at an uncertain point in time. WHAT GOES AROUND COMES AROUND. And nature has an impeccable timing for it.

Kabeer looked at me as if I was some traitor. That look at me was enough for me to read his mind. I knew I was in a pickle, but what I didn't reckon at that time was, my friendship with him and Radhika's proposal, both had to pay the cost of it. Meanwhile, I kept the phone in my pocket without saving the video.

"I don't need any kind of sympathy from anyone. I know very well what I did and why? You please stay out of it." Kabeer replied angrily to Radhika and pulled his hand back.

"Kabeer, saying NO to a right thing is considered as blunderful as saying YES to wrong one." She still tried to convince him thoroughly.

"Don't try to teach me what you aren't mastered in." He almost shouted. I hadn't heard such rude words from him to anyone ever, especially to a girl. He was really angry.

"Why are you taking everything in a wrong way, Kabeer?" she said changing her tone this time.

"I am like that and I'll always be like that. Do you have any problem with it?" He was totally delivering the arrogance with his words. He was really offended.

"Yeah sure, who the hell am I to say anything to you? You please go inside and keep continuing your good work, especially with that girl." Radhika bellowed, losing her cool finally.

"Don't include Aditi in it. She has nothing to do with this." Kabeer warned her.

"Hey, now don't pretend as if you have never dated her," Radhika said, completely ignoring his warning.

"So what, why are you reacting as if I have cheated on you?" He replied getting carried away in the heat of the moment.

Though he didn't bother to look at me with that 'traitor' glance this time yet I automatically went through the absolute embarrassment within myself. Kabeer funnily referred it as a 'DATE' that time when he told us, but I intentionally used the same term when I told about the same to Radhika. My intentions were wrong that time and KARMA had already come into the picture and made me realize it once again.

"Well done, Kabeer. You can boldly accept that you went on a date with her. You have accepted that you try to contact your ex-girlfriend by sending her messages. And even you love me too. But you are not ready to accept the fact that we can be together. Great! That's how you want to lead your life. You know what, you've really gotten addicted to this guilt factor. You've been living intentionally with it for ages and now you don't want to come out of it. But you yourself know that what you did was completely option-less and your decision was totally apt. Now carrying it as a burden for your lifetime is not pragmatic, but anyways leave it, who am I to say all these things to you? I'll not bother you again and I am really out of your life now." Radhika gave her farewell speech before stepping out of Kabeer's life.

Radhika then got as much infuriated as Kabeer. Like an eye for an eye, anger for anger couldn't serve the purpose. But the last two lines of her speech were just intended to show her anger and offense to Kabeer. Hearing those uproars and loud arguments, a professor from the nearby classroom stepped out. Aditi and company had also reached to the crime scene by then. Before the Professor would have advised them to go away, Kabeer himself left the place in anger without uttering a single word, as the footfall kept increasing. Nobody dared to ask anything to Radhika seeing her anger emitting red face. I, too silently shoved off afterward.

*

"He is just running away from reality. He is repeating his 'decision', this time for no reason." Radhika said hitting her fist on the table.

We were back in the canteen. The place where we planned the surprise was again witnessing us, but now as a failure.

"But you also went too far. I think you over-reacted." I shared my view honestly.

"What *yaar*, Vishu? You also saw him acting foolishly. I agree I got a bit carried away but he was totally illogical." She replied justifying her part.

"Leave it, we'll convince him later," I said trying to make her hopeful.

After Kabeer, it was my turn to shock Radhika. As Kabeer screwed up both, the plan and the her mood, I deliberately wanted to delay the shock process but her stubbornness didn't let me procrastinate. And therefore I ended up telling her everything which I conspired against Kabeer and which she unknowingly, was also a part of. I wanted to completely clean up my rotten mental system as I didn't want to carry forward that excessive baggage of an immature present to my hopeful future. And therefore, I confessed it all from the beginning to the end without pretending or saving myself at all. It was the only opportunity and I wanted to make most of it. Speaking the truth is a difficult job but living with a nasty lie is pure cowardice. I knew I had to pay heavily for it but paid right then was far better than living with the fear of losing uncertainly. ONCE COMMITTED TO FLY, NEVER DECIDE THE HEIGHTS. I did the same and did not try to restrict myself from speaking the truth and only truth.

"Never try to deliberately fit yourself in anyone's kitty otherwise you'll end up just being an identity of excess baggage," Radhika said to me before departing.

A lesson learned an hour ago by her and she felt like sharing the same with the person who needed to understand it more than her. It was applicable on both of us with the same intensity, but definitely with the difference in feelings. And I lost Radhika, perhaps for eternity.

*

"Kabeer, I am sorry, brother," I said as I entered the hall.

Yes, I was at DENCITY. I directly headed there, after confessing the bitter truth to Radhika. I knew it was awkward but it was the only possible way for me to clear everything from my end to Kabeer.

Whatever happened in the college became a trending topic in a very less time, though nobody was aware of the exact detail. It was just Kabeer and Radhika's loud argument which caught everyone's attention, which was, in fact, more than enough for the college to make sense from. The GANG enquired with me about it but I didn't reveal the complete secret to them. I was once bitten, twice shy and therefore I decided to directly come to DENCITY as on inquiring, Anshu told me that Kabeer was headed there after taking the keys of the apartment from him. I requested Anshu to call me up before coming to DENCITY as I was also going over there. I wanted to talk to Kabeer in complete privacy. Nonetheless, I was totally intimidated by seeing his angry avatar, yet it was the only correct way to justify my reason behind telling his past to Radhika. The only thing I did selflessly for someone didn't result in the way, it should've.

Kabeer didn't utter a word in reply. In fact, he didn't even bother to look at me. He was angry more than what I had thought and the situation had gotten much worse for me. What could you say to a person who was not even interested in responding? Forget responding, I felt he was not even considering me present there. I knew I was at fault be it unintentional but still I wanted some kind of response from him, no worry even if it was physical.

"Kabeer, slap me buddy, but don't be silent." I tried again and persuaded.

"Why!? Why should I slap you?" He reacted this time, finally breaking the ice.

"I know I shouldn't have told Radhika about your past." I gave him the motive to slap me.

"You know I shouldn't have told you to begin with. It would be far more appropriate." He retorted.

"Kabeer, don't say this bro. I just wanted her to know so that..." I was trying to explain my point but before that, he cut my justification midway and added his say in it.

"...So that she could shower her sympathy over me. Do you really feel that I need her to sympathize with me lifelong and I'll fall for her because of that sympathetic love?"

"I am sorry, brother. I didn't mean that." I quickly apologized to keep him calm.

"I've heard enough of you and your sorry, Vishesh. The day I joined the college until now, you always have this one word 'sorry' to tell for everything." He didn't approve my apology.

"Please Kabeer, don't get me wrong." I resisted.

"*You* got me wrong, buddy. My friendship with you was more of that like a brother. I've always tried to mentor you in the best way possible. Your curiosity made me believe that you could understand me better but like others, you too were obsessed with the HEADLINES only. I could've told about my past to Radhika way earlier but I didn't. Do you know why? It's not limited to my guilt or something, rather it was her beautiful memories that I hid from everyone and I want them to be with me forever. I need no one to come in my life and compel me to erase them, not even Radhika."

Kabeer got interrupted as my cell phone rang. It was Anshu's call, who respected my request and called me up before entering into his own home. I actually wanted some more time to spend with him in private so that he could speak out everything he was feeling and would accept my apology but then I also had to reciprocate the respect given to me by Anshu and hence I unwillingly asked him to come home as Kabeer also wanted it. Going against Kabeer's decision at that time, would be just like going against high tide waves. You know you would never find a right place to survive in friendship, afterward.

"I don't want to create any scene in front of Anshu and I think I could expect at least the same from you." He said as if it was some statutory warning and Anshu was the honorary Law.

I just nodded my head in vindication and left DENCITY before Anshu arrived.

****

CHAPTER 15

"SEE YOU NEVER, ALLIGATOR"

Anshu called me up the very next morning. I was still in bed as I didn't fall asleep until late that night or very early next morning. The whole night, I just thought about Radhika and Kabeer. The restlessness wouldn't buy me sleep. It was 04:11 am in the clock when I watched it last. Though I caught some sleep afterward yet I wasn't totally sleepy. I got out of that mild unconsciousness in the very first go as my cell phone initiated ringing. I grabbed it as fast as I could and switched on the light of the room. The clock mounted on the wall against my bed was displaying 06:30 am. I pressed the answer button of my cell phone and said 'Hello'. Anshu replied rashly from the other end and informed me that Kabeer had left for the ISBT KASHMERE GATE to catch some bus to his hometown DEHRADUN. He was in a total dilemma as Kabeer didn't tell anything exactly to him but assured to call him up after reaching. Anshu wanted to know the reality and hence called me up.

*

I was staying in DENCITY for last two weeks with Anshu. After Kabeer's sudden departure to his hometown, Anshu was all alone there and hence requested me to stay with him. I was going through a similar isolation and a guilt phase. Losing two best friends simultaneously was the worst thing that happened to me in those 4 years, I could confidently say that the I was the reason behind it too. I was totally unable to ruminate anything and that was transparently visible in my actions. I was half-hearted at everything and was incapable to cope with that unprecedented situation. I couldn't tell anyone about the miserable period of life I was going through. I desperately wanted to make everything exquisite between Radhika and Kabeer, but right then I needed to make things working for me first. Finals were just a couple of weeks away and I needed to fix a lot of things so that everything could be shaped up nicely. The first thing was my mood. I needed a change and hence I agreed upon staying with Anshu at DENCITY until Kabeer returned. And it was quite obvious that I had to give a logical reasoning to Anshu about what had happened that day among the three of us. I chose to tell the truth. Except for Kabeer's past life, I told almost everything to him. It was quite surprising for him to accept why Kabeer was angry over me and Radhika without any legitimate reason. I too acted clueless.

Being with Anshu helped me a lot to not overthink constantly. From studying to doing the household chores together, I tried to keep myself busy and it actually worked for me. I was feeling much better than earlier.

Apart from these activities, I still used to have plenty of time left to kill, because of which I completed my entire syllabus of the final semester in no time. I wasn't aware of the fact that I would become so studious at the end of that 4 year-long journey which was turning quite tough at the end likewise the start of it, except the study factor.

Meanwhile, placements had started and Kabeer as usual didn't turn up for them, irrespective of being informed by Anshu. He skipped all the placement interviews and didn't appear even after the insistence of Bhatiya Sir. However, by God's grace, I managed to get a decent job at ACCENTURE in GURGAON itself. It was the only delectable thing to happen to me in between all those traumas. Also, along with Sid and Lucky, Anshu too got placed at TATA CONSULTANCY SERVICES but as the company had clearly mentioned it in their offer letter that joiners would have to report at PUNE for the 3 months training programme, being the localities of Delhi, Sid and Lucky chose to opt out of it and decided to join some other well reputed companies at the NATIONAL CAPITAL REGION (NCR in Delhi). On the contrary, Anshu continued his decision of joining TCS as he was happy and ready to move there. Well, the raison d'etre for happily getting ready to go over there was his girlfriend, who was already staying in BANGALORE, which was hardly an overnight journey away from PUNE. We all were happy for each other and I personally wanted to celebrate the occasion grandly with my buddies of good and bad times, but then I realized that you cannot afford everything as per your convenience. Your personality is something which talks about you even in your absence and Kabeer's absence was really doing the talking for him. It was heartfelt and therefore we decided not to celebrate in his absence. Radhika had broken record by cracking all the placement interviews she faced and got multiple offer letters from various companies but then she eventually opted out in exchange for studying a Master's Degree.

It was time for the finals and hopefully, Kabeer would return. Although he had informed Anshu prior to his arrival, yet I wasn't completely sure if he would appear in the finals or not. No doubt, he was an extremely intelligent and wise fellow who knew better of what was best for him but simultaneously he had always been a shocking cum surprise element, just opposite to one's prediction. I was really happy that he returned. And I left DENCITY quite well in time, almost a day before his arrival. I wanted to deal sensibly with the situations along with him, this time.

*

Finals were over quite early and easily as we had to appear only for three theoretical examinations and lastly, the project interview remained. They got over easily also because I had prepared well in time for them and afterward also performed the execution too brilliantly. Meanwhile, Kabeer had not interacted with me even formally during the finals and I intentionally didn't try to bother him as I didn't want to interfere. I was waiting for the right time and right situation so that he wouldn't get me wrong again. I knew that the project interview was that right opportunity as we three had to appear together for it. And the countdown had already begun for me of that day.

*

"What was that? What were you trying to show inside?" Radhika almost shouted as we came out of the interviewer's cabin.

"Truth", Kabeer replied just in one word to her two questions which almost meant the same.

"Oh! Really, one who himself, is running away from the truth is helping others in seeking the truth." She taunted him citing their last conversation.

It seemed like it was not over between them. It wasn't a war but it was no less than one. Perhaps, Kabeer was pinched deeply. They say time is the best healer. It can heal everything. AGREED!!! But is it always so? I guess not always because it doesn't erase the scars every single time. Though scars don't pain yet they do establish as memory. And at times, memories hurt too bad.

He was perhaps in no mood of arguing with her and therefore he didn't even try to react. He totally ignored what she said.

"Is everything Okay with you? I mean at home." I asked seeing him silent.

"Totally", He again replied parsimoniously.

One word substitution was in all his responses to our questions. I wonder if he had learned it in all the days during his recent stay at home or he just wanted to keep things short so that we couldn't ask him anything that may propagate as a thread. He was completely predetermined about it and executing it exactly the way, he would have planned. We had left nothing much to ask and therefore fell silent. It rarely happened among us that we three were together and we had nothing to talk about. I hadn't expected it, at least not at our final day of the college. Kabeer was in no mood of sorting things out and he knew how to leave a mess of things perfectly.

"Kabeer, come inside. The Professor wants to have a word with you." Bhatiya sir narrowly opened the door of the cabin from inside and said.

"And you guys can go for your lunch. Please inform the next group to come after lunch." He instructed the remaining 2 of us.

We all followed his instructions instantly and moved in three different directions. Kabeer moved towards the cabin while Radhika directed herself towards the classroom. Seeing her going in the direction of the classroom, I automatically headed away from her. Well, she was already going away from me but I also had to go somewhere and therefore I decided to go to the canteen. It wasn't that I was really hungry but it was the only place I could think of going to. I was totally shaken by what had happened inside the interview room. I guess, everyone else present in the room had gone through the same feeling especially Professor Mrs. Bhatnaagar, the external interviewer who was aged around 55-60 years with partial grey hair and was continuously penetrating her experienced vision through the thick glasses that she had worn, as she looked curious enough like a child, to reckon what we were up to. Sitting next to Radhika after all that time since that confession at the canteen had already made me nervous and parallelly, the project thing was totally uncool. I had prepared well for the project interview so that I could answer anything if asked within those 80 pages of the project report but, 'worked practically on something and just read about it as a theory' are two completely different things. BEING CONFIDENT IS A QUALITY BUT FAKING CONFIDENCE IS A TALENT. I was trying to apply what Kabeer taught me once. And it was actually going fine from our end until Kabeer started receiving accolades from the interviewer. It seemed like he had also gone through the theoretical part of the project very well and therefore he started raising his doubts to Mrs. Bhatnaagar in the forms of whats, ifs and what-ifs, which was totally an alien concept to my not so thoughtful mind. But it was okay for me as long as he was able to keep her engaged and me out of focus of the question radar. And the best part was that she too seemed delighted in solving his queries contently. And in addition, Radhika too joined them in Q and A's and the whole concept of interviewing for the project had evolved into Group Discussion. The lady professor was quite impressed with both of them but more with Kabeer (perhaps she was mesmerized by that consistent childlike smile on his face) and hence she was in all praise for him. The twist in the tale came from here itself, as he foolishly told or purposefully confessed that he wasn't involved in the making of that project at all. When asked by the interviewer, what made him so straight to confess all at that point of time, he replied that he didn't deserve loads of appreciation he was getting for and then pointing at us, he gave all the credit of the project to us. Everybody was frozen for a moment or two after that revealing act and afterward, Mrs. Bhatnaagar asked us to leave the room and wait outside.

I was still waiting for my chance to once again apologize and speak my heart up to Kabeer. More than that, I was worried for him right then. His bitter truth at a wrong timing could cost him heftily. Though professor Bhatiya was along with him in that interview cum interrogation cum courtroom yet it was a case of 'intentional hit and surrender'. Well, neither I nor Radhika tried to counter-attack his confessing statement inside the room. What was done was done. Now I could only think of the things that had happened not in an ideal way and mourned over them for not shaping up ideally. Anshu, Lucky and Sid were already done with their interview as they all shared the same group and hence they had already left for home. Though I was also officially done with that of mine yet I decided to stay over there. I stayed there because I was seriously worried for Kabeer and his second personal interview. I also stayed over there as it was my last legitimate day in college as a student. Most probably, from the new and upcoming day onwards I was going to be an alumnus. Well, with that project interview, I had already become one. There was nothing left in the college for me except that 'no-dues clearance' form and few more documentation formalities. I had always thought of my last day in college would become as dramatic as that in of friendship based Bollywood movies. I even used to imagine myself crying while hugging those stupid people for the last time being the student of the same college. It took me about 1 hour to pass those 15-20 minutes and in between, I ordered a plate of samosa with coke twice. I could have ordered the same for the third time in a row if my cell phone hadn't displayed Kabeer's name on its screen while ringing. It was something unexpected to me. I mean completely getting ignored by him for almost a month and then out of the blue, getting a surprise call from him, had totally added a stamp of approval on my faith in miracles. Though we were together in that interview room, some couple of minutes ago yet he didn't bother to even look at me once and right now he wanted to talk to me over the phone. That was typical Kabeer. And that call from him meant that there was still something left between both of us, even from his side. Anyways, I took his call without any further ado and started a conversation with the usual 'HELLO'. He replied with 'HELLO VISHU'. Vishu, he addressed me by my pet name, which was also given by him, which meant that I was still left with some opportunities to win him over if only given a chance to let me explain. But before that, he told me to go to DENCITY as the GANG was waiting for me over there. I told him that I was in the campus itself and could wait for him to go along but he suggested me to go as it would take him longer to get out of there. I asked if everything was okay in the context of his project interview, he easily replied in 'nothing to worry'.

*

"Hi guys", Kabeer greeted everyone by waving as soon as he entered the hall.

We all waved back at him except Anshu who directly asked him for show-cause notice of keeping us waiting for too long.

"Sorry lads, I was with Bhatiya sir. Wow! Don't tell me, you all did this." Kabeer replied complimenting us on the arrangement done after being apologetic on getting late.

"Why did you switch your phone off? We tried calling you so many times." Anshu kept sticking to the point without being impressed with the appreciation.

"*Arre Baba*, I was with Bhatiya sir *na*. As, I am going tomorrow, I wanted to spend some quality time with him before final see-off." He replied very humbly.

"Going where?" Lucky asked interrupting their one to one conversation.

"Dehradun," He replied looking at Lucky.

"Tomorrow," Sid also participated in the conversation confirming the day of departure.

"Yep, in the morning", Kabeer answered specifically.

"Are you crazy?" Anshu again took-over the charge of the conversation.

"Almost, you know that very well roomie?" he winked and rushed towards his room.

Now that was Kabeer, totally unpredictable. He always used to take his time to sense the environment before taking any decision, either of holding on or moving on. And if once he was done, he was really done. Nothing could change his mind. And that time, he had decided to go. He decided to go but after a couple of hours. He decided to go but he let us know. In fact, he made sure that each and every member of the GANG should mark their presence at DENCITY for the last time and that was why he called me up over the phone, keeping aside whatever grudges he was holding for me or rather, he still made me feel privileged and blessed irrespective of whatever shit I tried to bring in his life, knowingly or unknowingly. We all really felt bad that he was going away just like that but then we still had the bunches of moments to live together and therefore we decided to live them grandly without spoiling the evening.

*

A carton of beer bottles was already finished about until an hour before midnight and the lads were quite okay by then. I mean everyone was in control especially Sid and Anshu unlike their earlier 'touch and go' performances. We had 6 more bottles to finish and at that point of time, it seemed like we were really running short of another three or four. After analysing the previous records and stats and also the individual's threshold capacity, 15 bottles looked more than enough for the GANG of 5 people who loved to have alcohol but were not addicted to it. But contrary to all that, the boys were performing better than expectation, beating their own previous records of boozing and afterward behaving unruly. And the speed with which Kabeer was destroying the existence of beer, made me feel like he would definitely complain about the shortage soon. Probably he might have forgiven me for my last blunder but then again I had given him another reason to get upset with me. He was already 2 bottles down and about to finish the third while the rest of us were miles away from his boozing sprint. And the more he was transporting alcohol to his blood, much friendlier he was behaving. Well, he had always been friendly with us but probably a month of silence between him and me had barricaded his display of feelings for me. Though he started behaving a bit eccentric, that was quite unusual with him, yet he wasn't out of his senses at all. In fact, he was making much more sense. And then he made us revisit all the nonsense we had been doing together for the last 4 years, through his spectacles of vision and we were almost literally rolling on the floor laughing. But even in that hilarious and 'alcohol-dominating-mind' condition, he didn't speak out anything against me. No complaints, no anger, just went with the flow. Perhaps, he had already fed it somewhere in his brain that he wouldn't need to discuss anything about what had happened between him, me and Radhika. Even Lucky tried to ask him about the same between those nonsense talks but he was really a hard nut to crack as usual.

"Why do you guys always love to talk about girls

especially when we get drunk?" Kabeer questioned Lucky and tried to divert the topic using his mind skills.

"And why do you always keep procrastinating, especially this topic?" Lucky questioned him back.

"Because I never find it relevant with our moments of gusto as we are here right now just because we love to spend time in each other's company. That's why we have never involved any girl in our *GANG*." Kabeer emphasized more on the 'GANG' while explaining his logic.

"But I don't think that Radhika is not a part of GANG. Though we don't consider her for our booze parties yet still she is important to us. And above all, we respect her." Lucky argued with a point.

"So when you are already so understanding, then what makes it so difficult to understand that I don't want to discuss about her right now, particularly when I am drunk?" Kabeer replied hollowly as his sheer point was to only evade the discussion.

"Then when will you speak up, after going home?" Lucky questioned further.

Lucky was in no mood of stopping quite contrary to earlier, as usually Anshu, Sid and I used to behave like that after getting drunk and he and Kabeer used to be the sensible ones. But for that last time, it seemed like we had exchanged our roles. We three were sitting silently. I, of course, had a reason but they too were behaving as if they got transformed into some voiceless species and hence we were attentively listening to their arguments with our shares of alcohol and butter chicken.

"Do you want me to waste this entire night in discussing over my past?" Kabeer forthrightly said coming to the point.

Kabeer hitherto reckoned that I would have already told the GANG about his ex-girlfriend and all, that was what I sensed from his way of expressions. But he wasn't aware of the fact that I actually didn't. I felt like interfering in their dialogue in order to avoid the complications but before me, Lucky commenced, "I don't know about which past you are referring to, but what I know is that Radhika loves you very much and you love her back, then why the hell you are playing dumb? I am totally clueless." Lucky said totally concerned over Kabeer's present life.

"Because there is no certain scope of ours as a couple and I just don't want to pretend that there may be some. I know I can't put my mother on extreme trauma in the name of convincing her for my relationship." Kabeer acquainted everyone, altogether with the half-truth but he didn't lie at all.

"No future. Are you sure there is nothing else except this? See I know that I am not as close as Vishu is to you but still we are best of friends and it really hurts me seeing that you as well as Radhika are hurt. You guys don't deserve to get hurt even by mistake." He replied emotionally.

Lucky summed it up like a true friend. Preparing a speech for an occasion like that and then delivering it, always looks stupid but naturally getting into a situation to speak one's heart is purely hypnotic. And Lucky had done just that. Why do they say that alcohol makes you do nonsensible things? Lucky made this statement questionable right then. I feel that alcohol just triggers some reserved feeling inside your heart which could either be sensible or otherwise nonsensible. Lucky and Kabeer were the examples of sensible ones while the rest of us belonged to the latter one.

"You are such a sweetheart Lucky. Come here." Kabeer said and brought him closer to himself as he was sitting next to him only.

"Ummmuaah, you are my brother like them." He kissed Lucky's cheek and said pointing at us. "And we are family. And in this family of ours, no one can replace any of the members, not even we."

Time to 'SPEAK-YOUR-EMOTIONS' had come and therefore we three stood up from our places and jumped onto them likewise to how football players celebrate with their teammates after a goal is scored. We tried to stay on top of them until the lowermost person started fidgeting. Unluckily, it was Lucky. I still remember the one who was sounding too sensible a couple of minutes before, had started abusing as we didn't get off of him. Alcohol makes you impatient and angry too easily, I also learned it from that incident. But thereafter, with Bhojpuri songs in the music player of a cell phone and bottles of beer in our hands, the night witnessed the GANG together for the last time.

*

I realized I slept too long as soon as I woke up next morning. It was around 10'o clock. Everyone else was up before me and I could hear their voices coming out of Anshu's room. I was lying on the floor in the hall as we all went off to sleep over wherever I remembered last, but it was totally looking messed up because of our last night's inhuman activities, so I reckoned that they went to his room as they got up. Apart from a mild headache which was obviously because of the hangover, I was feeling completely fresh. I realized that it was the first time I slept soundly since after the mess up with the relations and situations. College was over and so was Kabeer's acerbity towards me. In the end, it finally went fine. I was delighted. I was awake but I was still having the delectable feeling of being in a dream. I stood up quickly as I remembered that Kabeer had to go. Without losing a further second, I entered the room but then I got to know that I was already running late by millions of seconds. When the rest of the members of the GANG were traveling in their dreams, Kabeer had actually started traveling in reality. He was off to his destination without waking any of us. He loved to give surprises to people, but it came as a real shock for all of us. Though his absence was saying it all yet I asked to confirm how they got to know about his departure? Anshu handed me his cell phone in reply to my question. I saw a text message opened in it as soon as I held the cell phone. It was obviously Kabeer's. I read it in complete silence, in my mind.

"Hey Anshu, m going bro. Was unable 2 sleep, so decided 2 go a bit early. Didn't wanna disturb u guys, dats y

texting u. Sorry 2 all 4 sudden change of plan. Tc, of urself & my Juliet 2. Luv u all☺."

I read the message and scrolled down to check it's received time. 06:01, my curiosity was answered. I opened the recent dialled list and as expected, Kabeer's name was on the top which meant they tried to call him. Without confirming with them, whether they talked with him over the phone or not, I made a call to him. NOT REACHABLE was all I had to be settled with even after trying numerous times.

"We'll try later. He is traveling right now so maybe running out of signal or battery." Sid tried to console our restiveness with hopeful assumptions.

"Let's clean the hall first. It's too messy out there." I said to myself more than asking them to assist me and came out of the room looking for the broom.

I tried to keep the lads hopeful on getting a call from Kabeer's end but in actuality, I myself was feeling hopeless. My intuition and my gut feelings were strongly telling me that he had gone, perhaps for ever. And it all happened because of the one person, who for his own selfishness, messed up everything in his well-wishers' lives. Picking a broom up to clean the mess and dirt in the house is quite an easy and doable solution of reorganising the house but I actually wasn't able to find a remedy for what is really needed to be done when one has already created a lot of mess in his loved one's life and made his place untidy in their heart?

Kabeer made me feel that he had forgotten everything and forgiven me altogether but in less than 24 hours, my feelings were proved wrong. I realized that he had already planned all that what he later executed so neatly. He didn't want to create any scene at his farewell in any possible way and therefore he neither complained nor explained anything to anyone and kept doing everything exactly the way he always used to do. The rest of the members of the GANG were feeling delinquent because they weren't able to see him off for the last time while he left but to me, the guilt was of losing my opportunity (the last one, perhaps) to correct my earlier committed mistakes. And I realised that my mistakes were neither forgotten nor forgiven, on the contrary, I was forbidden from entering into his life again. I was absolutely sure that he had done all that for a purpose and as far as I could think, the purpose was not to be in anyone's reach. And if I was right then we could definitely do nothing and we really didn't deserve him. In a day or two everyone whom he was close to, came to know that we all were left behind by him only with his memories. I was not sure about others as I didn't discuss him (the real reasons of his sneaking away) anytime with them but I knew it very well that I acted the fault and searching for him in DEHRADUN, only to say a sorry is definitely not the intellectual and practical thing. At times, just a sorry is not enough in friendship and a sorry is nothing without putting efforts to mend the harm. Precisely, if to err is human then he is also meant to correct. That day I picked up a broom because a broom is supposed to do what it was invented for and hence that was how I got to pick up a pen to confess and tell the world that there was a KABEER BHAAGWAT who once used to have a GANG, a GENIE and a JULIET and together what nonsense they used to create in a place called DENCITY.

****

EPILOGUE

A happy ending is requisite of a fiction. But all in all, usually, in the end, there is an end either as an accomplishment or as regret. In my case, it is not so. And perhaps, that is why something unsettled inside me compelled me to pen down this book. I knew in the very best way that I wasn't politically correct on my part as a friend but then I realized my mistakes very soon. Yeah, it took me some time to find out the way to correct them but after getting motivated by one of my unusual friends. I didn't wait (for eternity) to let the things fell into the place by their own, instead, I tried to make the situation liveable at least for me. Well, the healing process starts right from the moment one stops worsening it.

'SORRY' is a small word and doesn't always express as much guilty as one actually feels. Kabeer and Radhika had their own justified reasons to leave me. But they really left me in pieces. They weren't together with each other either. I brooded a lot over contacting them but always found myself undeserving of their unconditional love and kinship. We really get everything that we deserve but only that much stays with us what we've earned truly. And I feel that I didn't earn them rather I took the two best things happened to me, totally for granted.

Moving-on is the basic concept of life and while making such transitions, care should be taken that distance should get covered and not created. I tried to move on too and honestly my new life was better than what I had asked for. I was learning professionalism and earning bucks at the same time. With new friends (actually colleagues) and a new lifestyle, I was really having a good time, but still, something inside me was nagging at me like an old but really painful thorn. I tried a lot to surpass my past guilt with my present success, but it is not so easy to undo the blunder from one's past, especially when he has already realized it. The only and the best way of getting out of the guilt is to take the necessary corrective action and not just keep sitting and brooding over it. In trust issues, for healing the victim's damage of 50%, it needs 100% efforts from the culprit to rebuild and reassure the same. And also, I was then completely able to understand and relate to the Kabeer's agony and guilt for his option-less decision, in a better way. But he wasn't tight-fisted like me. He didn't misuse the word 'move-on' to forget or run away from his guilt.

But in all that, Radhika appeared to me as unfortunate in terms of love and relationship. Loving someone thoroughly after officially entering into a relationship could be a commitment or talent but loving someone unconditionally and waiting for 4 years to listen 'I love you too' is more or less something like looking for the oasis in a desert. She risked it all for having Kabeer in her life and eventually lost herself. I won't say she was crazy and not practical rather I would love to define her as rare and real. Kabeer's prepossession ended him up losing two loving hearts, then and now.

Talking about the present, I don't know, how would he react when he comes to know about this book? I mean he could just sue me for divulging his secrets to the world but I think I have unveiled more of my secrets than his. So it's quite even between us, or so I would like to believe.

Lastly, I'll not use that word 'SORRY' again, instead I would love to say 'I LOVE YOU' to both of them. And when an introvert like me is obligated to admit and announce all his flaws and secrets in a confession-ish book then one can easily reckon the regression, agony, and guilt I have been through. But it's the same suffering which showed me the way and continuously pushed me to successfully pen down the most sparkly and relic moments of my life. And it's all because of that one moron Kabeer, who had always tried to bring the best out of me in his presence and now his absence has made me create a complete book. See, I have officially become an author.

I think, perhaps I don't even deserve him as well as Radhika, but I better know that they both can easily afford me anytime. And I am always hopeful for that ONE FINE DAY....

****

<u>*PRESENT DAY*</u>

<u>*RIGHT NOW IN THE FACULTY BLOCK*</u>

"TING-TONG, TING-TONG"

The bean bag over which the boy was sitting finally relaxed after some 3 odd hours as he went up to the door to acknowledge the bell. He kept the book over the table which was placed aside the bean bag. Meanwhile, the person at the door seemed more interesting in pressing the bell.

THE DOOR OPENED WITH A CREAKY SOUND

And the next few seconds went completely soundless.

"Hey, what are you doing here?" the person standing outside the door asked while removing her shades.

It was a girlish voice and her left hand was still placed over the bell-switch, though she had stopped pressing it. The boy didn't react at all in any way. Well, sometimes it's too hard to believe what you see.

"If you don't mind, Could I step in?" the girl asked again getting no reply to her earlier question.

"Oh! Yeah... sure," the Boy finally replied reviving his senses.

"Where is he? Is he still outside?" the girl asked curiously as she entered the house.

"Who, Bhatiya sir?" the boy replied in a question while closing the entrance door.

"Of course," The girl replied and started looking here and there inside the house.

"He wasn't here when I reached. He told me over the phone to wait." The boy replied politely.

"I too got a text from him regarding his absence. By the way, since when are you here?" The girl again asked making herself comfortable over the couch and kept her handbag on the table, coincidentally over that book.

"Some 3-4 hours, I guess. Would you like to have some water?" The boy asked out of courtesy.

"Yep, thanks. But I'll take it on my own. You better relax." The girl replied and smiled.

The girl stood up and without asking for directions, directly headed towards the kitchen and while going she requested him to make a call to Bhatiya sir by his cell phone as her phone's battery had already got flat. The boy's phone battery had also run down. The girl then suggested him to take out the phone and it's charger from her handbag and put it to charge. The boy obeyed her instructions.

"Owww, you still use this Nokia basic phone." The boy shouted as he put the phone on the charge.

"Old commitments," Girl retorted.

"And you please don't shout. I am neither deaf nor miles away. Your voice is very much audible to me." She again instructed him.

"Are you searching for water?" The boy, this time asked in his natural pitch while looking for Bhatiya sir's name in the phonebook as the phone started after boosting its power up a little.

"Just a minute, making some lemonade," Girl replied back from the kitchen with her reason.

"Haven't you saved Sir's contact?" The boy asked impatiently.

"Check in recent dials, na." Girl suggested.

"No, it's also not there. The last person you talked to is some Mihir." The boy replied hesitatingly after checking the dialled numbers.

"Before that?" she asked.

"Before him, you have only dialled to him for 1… 2… 3…, for three times in total." Boy counted the number of times she dialled the contact 'Mihir'.

"Spare him and just dial on my dad's number." The girl again directed him.

"Have you lost it? You want me to make a call to your dad and ask him for Bhatiya sir's number? Is this what you trying to say?" he almost shouted this time irrespective of the warning.

"No, not at all. All I am trying to say is my dad and Bhatiya sir are the same person. And if you remember, I told you that I address my maternal uncle as dad. So basically, your Bhatiya sir is my maternal uncle." The girl revealed the big secret very casually while stepping out of the kitchen and serving the glasses of lemonade.

"What? You never disclosed it." Boy shockingly said and almost jumped while sitting at his place on the couch.

His face was unable to hide those expressions which were totally narrating his present feelings.

"Neither did you, Kabeer." The girl said while deliberately sitting on the table placed against the couch. She called him with his name for the first time after so many years.

"Did you acquaint him with everything that had happened between us in college, Genie?" Kabeer asked getting freaked out and impatient at the same time.

She took a while to react but then totally ignored his question as well as his impatience. He kept on looking at her in the hope of some relevant response regarding his question but then perhaps, he read the expressions on her face in a better way, which didn't allow him to ask the same question again. He then tried making a call to the contact 'Dad' in order to break the monopoly of monotonous awkwardness but didn't get the relevant response from there either. Finally, he put a full stop on everything that he was doing to make the ambiance comfortable and switched himself to silent mode.

"So what are you doing nowadays and please don't call me with that name." Radhika broke the ice at last and asked in order to initiate the conversation again, applying do's and don'ts.

"Nothing much, helping mom in her restaurant's business." He replied strictly following the don'ts.

"Great! Always Mumma's sweet boy," She chuckled. "Well, I thought you would have become some Defence personnel by now." She extended her say.

Kabeer looked at her, smiled innocently and then looked down.

"And what's with you?" He asked in return.

"Completed Masters, now pursuing Ph.D." she answered.

"Following your Dad's footsteps," Kabeer retorted in his sarcastic way.

"Not exactly, but yes somebody once suggested that college campus is the best place to escape from this callous world. So you could say following his piece of advice." She too participated in that sarcastic conversation.

"Who told you that bullshit?" he said teasingly.

"Some saint Kabeer." She saluted him smilingly as she finished her statement.

"You still remember all that?" He asked being nostalgic.

"Fortunately, I never met with an accident affecting my memory otherwise I wouldn't have." She was totally nailing it.

"I don't know if I deserve to say it or not but I am sorry. I didn't care about your feelings and eventually broke your heart." He said being apologetic and emotional.

"It wasn't your fault completely. I too, over-expected." Radhika shared the blame.

"You know Radhika my life played some strange game with me. I have been living in guilt for last 9 years. Initial 4 years of guilt for her and afterward for you. I

have been in 'missing' mode all these years." He said and folded his legs.

"Did you meet her anytime?" She questioned with curiosity.

"No, not met exactly but she somehow contacted me over the phone as she managed to get my contact from somewhere." He said and swallowed the entire glass of lemonade in one go.

"So what was she up to?" she asked again.

"Great! Well, she was already into a relationship and sounded very happy. I said what I wanted to and sought her forgiveness. But it didn't matter to her anymore actually. She had already gotten over from the damage of the past, which was kind of relieving for me. But I still said sorry and assured her to never interfere in her life. I feel more relaxed and guiltless now." Kabeer told what he experienced.

"Didn't she ask you to hang on there? I mean, didn't you want her back in your life? After all, you felt that you really love her?" Radhika was on rapid fire.

"Radhika, it's good to create a castle of your own dreams but never try to be an architect for others. At least don't create chaos in their life with your limited views and situational needs." Kabeer donned the philosopher's hat.

"Now what's that?" She asked in confusion.

"Nothing, I always wanted to see her happy, be it with me or without me. This is actually what I have always

prayed for. And after so many years, I found out that she was actually happy. So I pulled myself back from there." He gave a literal illustration of his philosophical statement.

"And from there onwards, you started missing me. Isn't it?" she questioned.

"I've always loved you. It was a different kind of bonding with you. If that mess hadn't happened between us in the end, it would have always been impossible for me to avoid you for so long." He replied and added further. "Leave it. You tell me what are you up to? Must be in a relationship, right? You have become more beautiful than earlier."

"Really, you never complimented me like that earlier." She taunted.

"I never said I love you either." He riposted.

"So are you trying to say you love me? She tried to make the sum of Kabeer's statement.

"I am not trying anything. I am saying that I loved you." He made the equation simpler and took her hands in his hands.

"Is it because your ex-girlfriend doesn't love you anymore?" She replied with an unpleasant reason but didn't pull her hands back.

Kabeer who was looking at her beautiful hands while holding them, all of sudden let go of them and stood up quickly.

"Would you like to have some tea? Lemme make some actually." He asked and went to the kitchen straight away without waiting for her response.

In the very next moment, Radhika too reached the kitchen.

"Why do you always shy away from admitting the harsh truth? What keeps you scared of wearing your heart on your sleeve, even to me?" She asked and grabbed his hand from behind.

"If it really was so, then you would've already been contacted by me 4 years ago when she had officially gone off my mind." Kabeer turned towards her and replied to the last question asked by her in the hall.

"Why the hell didn't you contact me then?" she shouted in aggression.

"What do you think of me? Am I some opportunist? Not opportunist actually hypocrite, who better knows how to capitalize on other's feelings according to his needs. You know I could've accepted your proposal in college days only but I didn't want to enter into a new relationship with my heart full of guilt and mind brooding over my past. My equation with her wasn't clear to me, although it was already over between two of us. For me, she was still there in my notions, in my actions, everywhere. And moreover, it was me who left her because I didn't want any complications in my mother's life." Kabeer poured his heart out finally.

"So that means there is still no chance of our association as a couple?" she whispered.

"Aren't you in a relationship?" Kabeer asked surprisingly.

"Do I need to explain it, stupid?" Radhika said and clutched his shirt tightly with both her hands.

"How is that possible? I have seen your call logs. Who's Mihir?" Kabeer said and started backing away.

"Oh really, did you feel jealous of him?" she tightened her grip more over him.

"Where are you taking it to? I just asked because I felt so. By the way, it's your personal thing and therefore, you aren't bound to give any explanation. At least I don't need that." He replied as if he didn't care at all.

"See, how rude you are! You never make me feel that you love me." She hit with her fist at his arm and kept moving forward until Kabeer found the wall to block their movement further.

"Falling for you was all natural but how to love someone I learned from you, totally. You haven't waited for these 9 years alone, I too was in wait. I fell more in love with you as much as I got to know you. I didn't know if I would get any chance to see you again or not but I have always loved you with all my heart. I always had a hope regarding us and, it was sort of okay for me to live with those imaginations. I used to doubt my love whether it is true or......."

Radhika had also started pouring her heart out and wanted to say millions of words to express what she felt all those years without him. Kabeer, who was looking into her eyes without fail, too wanted to listen to all *that but perhaps that was not the right moment. It was probably not the right moment to communicate through the words but it was definitely the right moment to seal their lips and let their hearts communicate. Kabeer was the epitome of perfection and he knew the right thing to do at the right moment. He held her face within his hands and brought her closer to him. She wanted to say something but he didn't let her and kissed her on the lips. She tried again mumbling, and he again delivered a kiss, a passionate one and a tad longer from the previous one. She then decided to give up on words completely and just settled with a mischievous smile. He couldn't remain unaffected with that infectious smile in the middle of some really passionate osculation and tried asking about the naughtiness behind that smile but before he could have initiated it, she came on her toes taking over charge and delivered that long special kiss which turned Kabeer's mind blank and eyes closed. He embraced her tightly in response even after turning unresponsive.*

"Genie, you didn't tell me?" Kabeer said after a while as his unconscious mind became operative again. They were still hugging each other while she was slightly leaning more over him.

"What my AAKA?" she replied in the copybook style of the 'Genie' of 'Aladdin'.

"Who's that Mihir?" He just whispered.

She pulled herself a tad back so that she could see his face and then left a mark of love by softly biting at his cheek.

"My first friend and second cousin," she laughingly said.

*

FEW MINUTES LATER, STILL IN THE KITCHEN

"Kabeer, I need to show you something. You'll definitely get stunned." Radhika said putting her hands to blindfold his eyes as she was sitting on that marble slab of the kitchen.

"That book in your handbag." Kabeer who was standing facing her replied being partially blindfolded.

She removed her hands faster than light removes darkness. It seemed like, her each and every part of the body got shaken by the response he gave. With opened mouth and widened eyes, she herself got stunned. He didn't take time to wait for her next question and answered what she didn't ask but obviously wanted to.

"I saw it while taking the phone and charger out of your bag. Well, I too have the Xerox of it." He revealed the rocket science of the matter.

The secret divulged by Kabeer didn't impact her that much. Her reaction more or less remained like the earlier. Seeing that book wasn't a big thing but knowing the content was, and the way he responded had apprised her that he knew about that book in the best way. She was still drowning in the ocean of curiosity. Kabeer's presence at B-13, Faculty Block was a sheer coincidence or well-planned strategy, she was unable to figure it out. But he figured it out instantly whatever disturbances of notions were going on in his Genie's head. Though he too was totally incognizant of that master plan, which he somehow became a part of, yet he hitherto, had almost solved that mystery in his head. The only missing thing was confirmation, the confirmation from the planner of RadhiKabeer's reconciliation story. Anyways, she remained in an absolute dilemma until she got to understand that how everything was planned by her dad as Kabeer narrated the entire story of how he got to read the same book today itself. It wasn't a million dollar question for them to reckon that who penned it down? But the real question was why? Yes, of course, it might be written only for them to make them realize that they really love each other a lot and it was planned in such a way that they made sure that both of the lovers must read it completely before confronting each other. And in the heat of the moment, they couldn't resist their frozen differences to melt in their true feelings for each other. And if it was so then the 'planners' really executed their plan very beautifully. Meanwhile, Radhika who was totally in shock a couple of minutes ago had fully shifted her focus from present to future as Kabeer apprised her with the expected possibilities of the question why it was planned so?

"Kabeer, I'll ask dad to talk to your mother about us. Or do you think I should personally talk to her? Do you feel I could win over her?" Radhika said with the utmost innocence.

Kabeer who was cuddling her asked mischievously as he ran his fingers through her hair, "Ahaan! And what will you say to her?"

"I'll say that I love your son very much and I can't live without him. Please accept me as your daughter. I'll never let you down." She replied very cutely.

"Really, And what if she still won't approve us as a pair? He asked doubtfully.

"I'll die without you baby. I really will. Till now, I had a reason to live without you but now when you yourself accepted me, I cannot afford to lose you anyhow." She choked while speaking and whimpered.

Kabeer instantly unhugged her and took her innocent face in his hands.

"Mom knows everything, Genie. In fact, I told her about all that happened in my life. Earlier she got upset of me a bit but then when she brooded over it, she very soon, realized the trauma her son went through all alone. She slapped me for hiding all that from her and then cried along with me. She couldn't see me sacrificing my happiness for some bizarre promise I made to myself. She knows that I love her too much and so does she. She then asked me about my proclivity. I told her about you and even showed your photograph. And you know what, she liked you." Kabeer said wiping out the tears off her face.

"Did she really like me or are you saying all that just to please me?" she looked at him and asked doubtfully.

"Genie, why would I lie? Actually, she loved you. In fact, everybody loves you." He replied.

"And you?" She questioned again.

"What do you feel?" he questioned back.

"Just tell na?" she said being teary-eyed.

"More than me," He whispered before locking his lips with hers, one more time.

TING TONG!!! TING TONG!!!

The doorbell squealed and updated the presence of somebody at the door. The 'somebody' whom the insiders had been waiting for since their arrival and in fact, they actually came over there only to see that 'somebody'. But because of some unforeseen conditions, some deliberate coincidences and the air containing more percentage of love than that of nitrogen, oxygen and even pollution, in that house, the wait turned out into a beginning of new innings for old lovers. And when the old love gets propelled, one thing automatically leads to another. Lips on the lips are as valuable and necessary as the tears in the eyes. Well, they had already witnessed tears in each other's eyes a few times in the past but that lips over lips was something new to them in terms of experience and therefore the two kissing-hugging took two more rounds of bell to ring to finally be separated followed by making themselves look normal and then to acknowledge the guest, who actually was the only resident of that apartment.

"FROM THE PROFESSOR'S SECRET B OX"

No, that wasn't my plan. It just worked the way I thought it should and therefore it was Almighty's plan. I accept, I insisted Kabeer a tad bit more to come over to Delhi after that long break but then I also felt that somewhere deep down inside he had given me that privilege of asking for more from him. That was why he chose to be in touch with me all those years when he literally vanished from every other person's life in the college. On the contrary, he never shied away from gathering information regarding them and their whereabouts through me. Well, I also never let any of them know about this secret until the end. But at the end, there should be nothing tacit. And as I wanted to make the execution perfect, I couldn't afford to take a risk of even an iota. Kabeer had to be there and I managed to get him on the roller-coaster. After all, we put in an ample amount of effort to make things impeccable.

This GEN-X has something special and different with them. Like every generation, their views and approach to the matter are slightly different from their predecessors. But their urge to make everything right is absolutely commendable. Impulsiveness is their analogue, but then they also wish to endure their parental traditions and cultures. They seem progressive but sort of conservative in some selective ways, especially these kids of late 80s and early 90s. They are the perfect blend of old Indian values and avant-garde. Unlike traditionalists, they prefer to promote realistic and practical things along with the acceptable cum logical rituals. They want their family to be their support system for their career as much as they want their career to support their family. They *are as good in sacrificing their happiness as they are stubborn for their passion. Well, life cannot be idealistic, if it is realistic. And therefore a small deviation is always allowed.*

Well, I am a teacher as well as a parent, a teacher by choice and a parent by chance, but a fortunate one in both the cases. And when I use the term 'Fortunate' then it really has something to do with my life. As a person, I love reading people's minds and psychologies. If I say I have literally become a psychogalvanometer, then it is no exaggeration. Being in college provides me a hell of a lot of people to observe and interact with, mostly these young guns.

Though I was completely aware of the pros and cons of Radhika's personality who had grown up in front of me, yet she is someone who helped me a lot in gelling up with the term 'Today's Youth'. God didn't bless me with my own offspring but coincidently he gifted us with Radhika. She remembered everything about her parent's tragic death but then the way she assimilated us as a part of her life, it never let us feel like we were child-less ever. From schooling to college, she never missed an opportunity to make us proud of her. And in fact, she was the one who compelled me to hide my identity of her father in college. And, the logic was she didn't want to get misconstrued as a favoured pupil. Honestly, she was candid and so was I and therefore I agreed on that hidden-identity thing. She has always been forthright and it was her topmost trait that contributed in evolving herself as a self-made person. Now there's something interesting about her which I would like to share. I really don't know whether we practiced good parenting with her or not, because like every parent we tried to do everything for her from pampering to protecting her as she was the life of the house.

But with her age, she grew as a person more. She didn't choose a laid-back attitude for herself, instead, she wanted to be liable. She was a curious spearhead who always made us back up her choices and decisions because of the trust she earned among us. And she didn't even try to misuse the term 'independence' in any which way. For her, independence was not hypocrisy and therefore she was very well aware of her limits. She was and is a fighter and can do anything once she is committed to it. But these two boys, whom she was closely associated with, are tremendously blessed especially Kabeer. He is totally gifted, a composed leader, a team player, sensible, handsome, extremely intelligent as well as witty and easy to talk with, kind of all in one. Generally, a man is known by his passion but a gentleman is defined by his compassion. And like my daughter, I also started liking this passionate gentleman ever since he was introduced to me. And when I got to know about his past through Vishesh, I automatically started respecting him, definitely a silent sacrificer who was always ahead of his age. He was so influential that he unknowingly polished Vishu's character. Though Vishu too was way talented and capable but being continuously in the disciplined company of Kabeer, his talent turned into ability. He found too much space to evolve, such that in the midst of the process itself, he felt like competing with his inspiration, that was Kabeer. But then maturity is something one gets by paying for it and as I said, Kabeer was gifted so he paid for it a bit early on but Vishu was going parallelly with his age, which was quite okay.

Let me share one more secret with you. This is about Kabeer, the actual secret box and legitimately the owner of a quite famous and spacious three-storey restaurant known as

'AAGANTUK' in DEHRADUN, which is obviously run by his mother as she loves it just as her children. But Kabeer is a good aide like always and therefore he helps her in running as well as in promoting their restaurant business in every possible way. But I didn't buy that he settled down so easily after giving up on chasing his dream. So one day I decided to go to his hometown to do a reality check and I was fascinated to witness that, 'AAGANTUK' was actually one of the most talked about things of the town. More than that, it has literally become a landmark to get and give directions inside town. Before stepping inside, I made sure by making a call to Kabeer to ensure that he wasn't at the restaurant. And I was fortunate to meet that graceful lady. I felt no wonder why Kabeer is so blessed. Like mother, like son. That day, I inferred that Gravity has nothing to do in keeping us grounded. She was an earthly soul, who after reaching zenith from cipher, obviously against all odds, had nothing to brag about. She was the epitome of simplicity and therefore undoubtedly, I felt touched. I revealed her my identity and my intentions. And from the very next moment, she recognised me. It seems that Kabeer had already boasted of me a lot to her, so it didn't take us time in connecting soon. And there I got to know all the big hush-hush about this boy from his current love life to professional life. He, who after opting out of his dream, is helping the 'aspirers' to see their dreams. Kabeer started it off from taking tuitions for school kids on a comparatively lesser fee, as he wanted to see himself involved and do something productive of his passion. His idea of starting the coaching centre was certainly not to earn a hefty amount of money. But altogether he also knew it in the best way that, things for free in this world are always either taken for granted or mistaken for being unserious. So instead of going

for 'social service for free', he chose to do 'social service on a low fee'. And his idea worked, by the way. Along with studies, he started taking sports coaching classes for his students without charging a single additional penny for it. Earlier he just used to make the kids play by taking them to the nearby ground but as the number of students kept increasing, as the duration of the coaching progressed, so thereafter he formed a sports basic coaching class. Sports is something, he was totally mad about and therefore it needs no explanation to tell what a man can do when he works on his passion. Study plus sports for younger kids at one place was quite rare and definitely a convenient offer especially for parents and on a less than a reasonable fee, it was quite obvious for them to give it a try for once. Kabeer wasn't aware that his coaching class would get flooded with so many students and therefore his classroom (which was his own room at home) felt small. He thought of forming batches to take the class shift-wise but then that was also not possible for him to spare time as he also had to take care of his restaurant every now and then. He really wanted to suppress the exponentially increasing strength of his class but he was also not able to refuse the innocent kids who themselves wanted to join him enthusiastically. Kabeer was very fond of kids and vice versa and therefore he came up with an idea to use the third floor of his restaurant to teach his young students. The third and uppermost floor was specially designed like a banquet hall so that customers could reserve it in order to celebrate birthdays and parties, but as most of the times it used to remain unreserved, Kabeer started taking his classes over there. In barely a couple of years, 'AAGANTUK' became more famous apart from for its food and hospitality. And it was purely Kabeer's passion and obsession which ignited with the hard work and smart works, resulted in a pleasant aroma of fame. He then took an unconventional but a really giant leap forward by taking the bold and brave decision of starting motivational classes as he really wanted to focus solely and completely in shaping up the character and personality of young minds towards atheldom. His logic was very simple and clear that one can seek academic knowledge from school and other coaching centres very easily but no one considers to teach moral values and ethics as strictly as they are supposed to be, which is as eminently required in life as an individual's career. Without generosity, a heart is nothing more than a mere blood pumping organ. Because of his personal interest and out of the box thinking, he started doing what he felt he was good at. Moreover, he wasn't doing any commercial business in which he would get disheartened if his idea wouldn't deliver as per expectations. It was a thought of betterment and for betterment. Unlike the academic tuitions, he did not stop his sports coaching classes as he always says that a team sport teaches us teamwork, better planning & strategies, intense pressure absorption, making effective decisions and most importantly teaches us how to be happy in other's happiness. And life more or less is a game of sport where you achieve, you lose, you give, you get it back, you get injured, you get an award.

All in all, Kabeer is really happy at what he is doing. I guess he is happy more because he is not over-ambitious. He knows happiness lies in living what you are passionate about and constantly working towards the accomplishment of that dream. And having one's family beside him in such a sort of journey provides actual happiness. We all thought that Kabeer had given up on his dream of joining the Indian Army and serving the motherland but no, we all were wrong. We were just expecting his dream to come true exactly the way as how he made us see it, but, moving a step ahead of his dream, he started doing his bit to serve the nation in another way. As he said in my motivational class way back then that '**an improved mentality is not only an asset for individual grooming but also for the nation'**, so did he execute his action. And he is still continuing his good deeds for the amelioration of the individual as well as the future of this nation.

WORDS DON'T ONLY HAVE MEANINGS, THEY HAVE VALUES TOO. I learned it from Kabeer that day. Earlier I had thought of meeting him but then I requested his mother to keep it as a secret as I decided to return without letting him know that I was there. He had already taken his call and now it was my turn to take my call and I promised myself that particular day that he would surely get the reward for his selflessness or passion or perseverance or love, whatever he feels apt to say.

IF LIFE IS ALL ABOUT A CONTEST THEN TRY TO CONQUER THE RELATIONS. REALIZATION is the only and best teacher to guide one. And therefore when Vishu realized his mistake, he tried everything to correct it and finally he stepped out of his comfort zone. This book is the proof of it.

YES! I gave him the idea of writing a book on them, but it's completely his perseverance and hard work which resulted in such a lovely book. Well, I didn't tell him about Radhika and my relationship with her until he handed me the final manuscript as I really wanted him to write the exact honest details, not the altered one. Though being a father, it was quite bizarre to read one's own daughter's romance but being a true pioneer,

I needed to defy the law of hypocrisy and advise true and best things at least to one of my three special students, who wrote an entire book over the other two. And in the whole process, a father of none became the 'fortunate' father of three.

"PROLOGUE"

(Because it's the re-start of my life after gaining my soul-mates back)

Making eye contact with someone, you always craved to meet but actually meeting them after the blue moon, is one of the hardest jobs to do. No matter how much closeness and what sort of bonding you used to share at a certain point of time, it always takes time to come out of the mask of formalities.

Kabeer hugged me and made it easy for me to react comfortably. I have been waiting for this moment for ages with all the butterflies in my stomach and therefore I hugged him back firmly. The best thing about old friends is that it needs only one hug to revive the friendship which makes you forget every bitter thing of the past. While his hug was formatting the trash and securing healthy database of my memory, my heart automatically dethroned the 'trojan of guilt' inside it. Meanwhile, Kabeer realized my restiveness and hence whispered into my ear," c'mon, don't think of crying over here otherwise I'll let everyone know about that unprecedented dance of yours at the canteen." I, who was about to move to tears suddenly burst into laughter. He placed a kiss at my shoulder and cheered me up," JIYO RAJA." And there, we were back to the genre of 'NONSENSE' again.

Radhika and Kabeer were totally taking it as a prank that the manuscript they read had already got shaped up into a book and been published too. But when they finally realized that it was not a joke anymore, they almost tried to kill me. After getting ruthlessly whipped with fists, shoes, sandals etc., I realized that a phone call with a sorry could also have done the job. I really cursed the moment when I went to seek advice from Bhatiya sir and he didn't even reveal his relation with Radhika until the end.

Radhika literally made me touch her feet as a punishment for making her personal thing public and Kabeer shot the entire video of that feet-touching incident, teasing me.

Anyways, I guess all this is turning into a blessing in disguise for me as the book published with the tragic ending has given me an opportunity to write the sequel i.e. "Life after book launch". Earlier when I started writing this one, I wasn't even sure of completing it. But then I managed to complete it, got it published and finally launched it at the same place where I actually lived it. In the process, the actual motto of penning it down also was justified and rewarded as Radhikabeer's love was just not restricted only to a story and finally took off after half a decade. Quite otherworldly! Isn't it? From 'degrading the value of friendship' to 'leaving no stone unturned in reviving the same friendship', I rediscovered myself. A beautiful smile automatically appears on my face every time I realize that the mission has been accomplished. Though I am not able to see it literally, yet I can bet my bottom dollar that it must be truly beautiful, the same as Radhika and Kabeer never fail to deliver. After all, I could feel it with all my heart which also happened to help me in inferring with a thoughtful statement. God blessed humans with a mind along with another mind commonly known as 'Heart'. This Heart is Almighty's own piece of mind which always keeps supplying us with the best advice and ideas every now and then. Sometimes they get a match with that of our mind and sometimes not. Sometimes, they appear too risky and unsure and therefore we totally ignore them and rely more on that given by our minds. But at situations like what I was in, where my mind really fell short to reckon what was exactly needed to do to come out of it, my heart made me believe to work on this idea. Honestly, my mind was doubtful over it until the end but then my mind was proved wrong with that of Almighty's, BECAUSE GOD IS NOT SUPPOSED TO ERR.

Well, we will continue this discussion later on. It's already 23:55 in my laptop cum watch and I really need to shut it down as Radhika is continuously instructing me to do so, whisperingly. All lights are already off in B-13, FACULTY BLOCK as GANG has been waiting eagerly for clock to strike 12 so that we can wish our darling professor a very happy birthday who is totally incognizant of the upcoming surprise event.